PENGUIN BOOKS

FAREWELL TO FAIRACRE

Miss Read, or in real life Mrs Dora Saint, is a teacher by profession who started writing after the Second World War, beginning with light essays for *Punch* and other journals. She has written on educational and country matters, and worked as a script-writer for the BBC. Miss Read is married to a retired schoolmaster and they have one daughter. They live in a tiny Berkshire hamlet. She is a local magistrate and her hobbies are theatre-going, listening to music and reading.

Miss Read is the author of numerous books, which have gained immense popularity for their humorous and honest depictions of English rural life, including, most recently, *Celebrations at Thrush Green* and *Farewell to Fairacre*. Many of her books are published by Penguin, together with six omnibus editions and an anthology, *Country Bunch*. She has also written several books for children, including The Red Bus series for the very young (published in one volume by Puffin as *The Little Red Bus and Other Stories*), a cookery book, *Miss Read's Country Cooking*, and two volumes of autobiography, *A Fortunate Grandchild* and *Time Remembered*.

MISS READ

FAREWELL TO FAIRACRE

PENGUIN BOOKS

PENGUIN BOOKS

Published by the Penguin Group
Penguin Books Ltd, 27 Wrights Lane, London W8 5TZ, England
Penguin Books USA Inc., 375 Hudson Street, New York, New York 10014, USA
Penguin Books Australia Ltd, Ringwood, Victoria, Australia
Penguin Books Canada Ltd, 10 Alcorn Avenue, Toronto, Ontario, Canada M4V 3B2
Penguin Books (NZ) Ltd, 182–190 Wairau Road, Auckland 10, New Zealand

Penguin Books Ltd, Registered Offices: Harmondsworth, Middlesex, England

First published by Michael Joseph 1993
Published in Penguin Books 1994
3 5 7 9 10 8 6 4 2

To Eileen and Mike
with love

Contents

PART THREE
Summer Term

PART ONE

CHRISTMAS TERM

CHAPTER 1

Term Begins

The first day of term has a flavour that is all its own.

For one thing, it invariably dawns fair and bright, no matter how appalling the weather has been in the days preceding it.

In fact, the last two weeks of the school summer holidays had been cold and rainy, washing out any plans for picnics or gardening which I had made. As headmistress of the neighbouring village school of Fairacre, I had hoped to spend the last weeks of my summer break in tidying the garden before the autumn leaves swamped the place. Now such plans had been thwarted, for I must return to my school duties.

On this particular September morning, the view from my kitchen window was bathed in sunlight. Dew sparkled on the lawn where a thrush hastened hither and thither with an ear alert for worms below. Spiders' webs decorated the hawthorn hedge with medallions of silver lace, and the branches of the old Bramley apple tree were bowed down with fruit.

Beyond this spread Hundred Acre field dotted with sheep, and farther still the misty bulk of the downs against the sky.

I was lucky to live in this pretty downland village of Beech Green. Luckier still to live in the cottage which was

now my home, for it had been left to me on the death of a
dear friend and colleague, Dolly Clare.

She had lived there for most of her long life, arriving at
the age of six with her sister Ada, and her parents Francis
and Mary Clare. It was Francis who had rethatched the
cottage, and some of his tools had been used, years later,
by a young thatcher who inherited them.

When Dolly told me, in the last years of her life, that she
had left the cottage to me, I was overwhelmed at such generosity.

All my working life I had lived either in lodgings or in
the tied school house at Fairacre. More prudent teachers
had invested in property, as I should have done, but
somehow I had never got round to taking out a mortgage,
and the years slipped by as I enjoyed my rent-free time as
headmistress of Fairacre school.

But a few years earlier, my former assistant and dear
friend had left me this lovely home, and I have never
ceased to be grateful.

The village of Beech Green is some two or three miles from
Fairacre, and Dolly Clare had cycled there and back each
school day for many years. I was luckier and had a car to
shelter me on my daily journey. We get plenty of blustery
winds in this open area, and Dolly must have had many rough
journeys in her time, but I never knew her to be late for school,
and she always looked immaculate in the classroom, no matter
how severely the elements had battered her on the way there.

The kitchen clock said eight o'clock. It was time I tore
myself away from all the delights before me, and set off for
a new term.

Tibby, my fastidious cat, oozed through the cat-flap and
surveyed my offering of the most expensive cat food on
the market with considerable distaste, before walking away,
and I made my way to the garage.

The morning air smelt as seductive as the flowers which scented it.

It was sad to have to leave the garden, but there was no help for it.

Term had begun, and I must be on my way.

At first sight, Fairacre school looked much as it did a hundred years ago. A low one-storey building with Gothic windows and porch, it did its Victorian best to imitate St Patrick's venerable pile near by.

The playground was dappled with sunshine and the shadows of lofty trees in the vicarage garden next door. In one corner stood the pile of coke which would soon be needed for the two tortoise stoves inside.

A few children were already rushing about in the playground, and one or two of the most effusive galloped up to throw their arms round my waist in exuberant greeting. Such affection would be somewhat muted, I knew, as the term progressed and we all settled down to our usual workaday relationship, but it was very cheering to be greeted as if risen from the dead, and I was glad to see them in such good spirits.

My curmudgeonly school cleaner, Mrs Pringle, was not quite so welcoming.

'That skylight,' she told me dourly, 'has been up to its old tricks again.'

I thought that Mrs Pringle was also up to her old tricks, damping any enthusiasm she encountered on this bright new morning. The skylight was an enemy, of many years standing, to us both.

'Anything special?'

'All this 'ere rain has done its worst,' she informed me with satisfaction. 'Dripped all over your ink stand, run under the map cupboard, and nearly got to *my stoves*.'

Here her voice rose in a crescendo and her jowls grew red and wobbled like a turkey-cock's. The two tortoise stoves at our school are the idols of Mrs Pringle's life, and she ministers to them with love and blacklead and all the considerable power of her elbow.

'I'll get Bob Willet to have a look,' I promised her.

Bob Willet is our school caretaker, sexton and grave-digger at St Patrick's church, and general handyman to whoever is in need of his services in Fairacre.

He is an expert gardener, a steady church-goer and a good friend to all. Our village, without Bob, would lose its heart.

But Mrs Pringle was not to be placated so easily.

'I can't be everywhere at once. I come up here twice a

week regular all through the holidays, and there's not many school cleaners as can say the same. I've worked my fingers to the bone for all these years, as well you know, and for what thanks?'

I looked at Mrs Pringle's fingers which were nowhere near the bone, but rather resembled prime pork sausages.

'Well, I thank you. Often.'

'But do those dratted kids?'

At this point a posse of the dratted kids appeared in the doorway, beaming broadly.

'It's bell time, miss. John Todd says it's his turn, but he done it last morning of term.'

'*Did it*,' I corrected automatically. Not that it would make the slightest difference, but once a teacher always a teacher.

'Anyway,' I added, 'it's a new start today, so Eileen may ring the bell.'

Term had undoubtedly begun.

Ever since I arrived at Fairacre some years ago, we have had the threat of closure hanging over our heads.

It is a two-teacher school and seems to have been so for most of its long life. When I came, the numbers were between thirty and forty on roll, but early log books show that occasionally the school numbered around a hundred pupils.

In those days families were large. It was nothing to have four or five children from the same family under the school roof at the same time. Also, of course, children stayed until the age of fourteen, but in these rural areas it was not uncommon for them to leave at twelve if they had been offered a post. Most of the boys went into farming, and most of the girls into service.

During my time, my schoolchildren ranged in age from five to eleven years, and after that they proceeded to George Annett's care in the school at Beech Green where they stayed until fifteen.

The plight of our falling numbers over the years was a constant headache, and only a year or two earlier they had fallen to about twenty. My assistant teacher, Mrs Richards, who taught the infants, and I thought that the outlook was gloomy.

But amazingly help was at hand. Two new houses in the village were bought by a charitable housing trust, part of the Malory-Hope foundation, the brain-child of a much-loved local philanthropist. One house was already occupied. Here a married couple in their forties were in charge of four children, the youngest five years of age and the eldest ten. All four had been at Fairacre school now for one term, and were welcomed by Mrs Richards and me, as well as all those who had the welfare of our school at heart.

The other house was awaiting five children, but one would be a baby. Nevertheless, the thought of four more children, of school age, to swell our numbers in the near future was decidedly heartening.

There had been some plumbing problems with the second house which had held up the arrival of the second family, but we all hoped that we should see our new pupils by half term, at the end of October, or certainly by Christmas.

The Trust had been set up, some years earlier, by a wealthy and philanthropic business man. It began as a housing scheme for the orphans of men who had served in the armed forces, and today it still gave such orphans priority. But as the Trust's work expanded, other children were accepted, and the founder's basic desire for family units was respected. Not more than five, and usually four, children were looked after by a married couple in a small home. They attended the local schools, and took part in general activities, and the regime seemed to work admirably.

I must admit that when the news broke in Fairacre that two families would be housed in the Trust's latest acquisitions, there were a few misgivings from the older inhabitants. Mrs Pringle, of course, was one of the gloomier forecasters.

'I've heard tell as some of these kids come from towns.'

'What's wrong with that?'

'Remember them evacuees? All town lots they were. And brought no end of trouble. Head lice, fleas, scabious —'

'Scabies,' I corrected automatically.

'As I said,' continued Mrs Pringle, undaunted. 'Not to mention bed-wetting and *worse*.'

'Well, these aren't evacuees, and are being properly brought up. Frankly, I'm looking forward to them, and so are the children.'

'You'll regret it,' said my old sparring partner. 'Mark my words.'

But her dark forebodings had not come to pass. The four new pupils had settled into Fairacre school very well, were accepted by the children with the easy camaraderie of the young and, to my mind, were a very welcome addition to the establishment.

The golden September weather continued. The children still wore their summer clothes and complained of being 'sweatin' 'ot, miss', but continued to rush around the playground, and occasionally up and over the coke pile when they thought they were unobserved, so they did not get a great deal of sympathy from me when they pleaded exhaustion from the weather conditions.

But I relished this balmy spell of weather. We had some lessons out of doors, particularly those which involved reading, either by me, or on their own.

Sometimes I suspected that the combined siren voices of a distant tractor driven by someone's dad, the cawing of the rooks above us in the vicarage trees and the humming of innumerable insects around us took more of the children's attention than the printed pages before them. But this did not perturb me greatly. They would remember those golden moments long after the stories had faded from their memory.

Sometimes I took my class for a nature walk. This was always exhilarating, particularly when we traversed the village street on our way to the chalky paths of the downs. A mother, on her way to see Mr Lamb at the Post Office, would greet us warmly. A distant tractor would be pointed out enthusiastically.

'My dad's over there. They're havin' swedes in that field this year.'

Someone would wave from an upstairs window.

'My gran,' said Ernest, waving back. 'She has a nap on her bed after dinner.'

Such encounters were very cheering, but I could not help noticing that there were far fewer people about in the village than when I first came to Fairacre years ago.

Now it was the norm for both parents to go to work, and nowadays at a distance, travelling by car. Certainly, both parents had worked in earlier times, but usually within walking distance of their houses.

Mr Roberts, our local farmer, probably employed eight or ten men when I knew him first, and their wives helped at the farm house or at nearby large homes with domestic work. Usually it was part-time work for the wives, for they arranged matters so that they could be at home at midday to dish up a meal for their husbands and any of the family who were at hand. A number of my schoolchildren went home to a midday meal when I first started teaching at Fairacre. Nowadays all stayed to school dinner. It was a sign of the times.

A few hundred yards beyond the edge of the village, a path led upwards to the downs. The first few yards were shaded by shrubby trees. The wayfaring trees grew here, their oval grey-green leaves encircling the masses of white flowers so soon to turn brown and change into autumn berries. Brambles clutched at legs, their fruits already forming into hard green knobs, and here and there a second flowering of honeysuckle scented the air.

But as we ascended we left the scrub behind, and found ourselves in the high windy world of true chalk downland.

We sat puffing on the fine grass and enjoyed the splendid view. There were pellets of rabbit droppings around us among the tiny vetches and thymes of the grassland, and the small blue butterflies which inhabit chalky places fluttered about their business, ignoring intruders.

We pointed out to each other various points of interest.

'There's the weathercock,' said Patrick. 'It says the wind's in the east.'

'Soppy!' commented John Todd. 'You be lookin' at his tail.' An ensuing scrap was quelled by me.

They noticed washing blowing on a distant line, a train making its way to Caxley station some ten miles away, and a herd of black and white Friesian cows behind Mr Roberts' farm house.

Was this, I wondered guiltily, really 'A Nature Walk'? Was it, more truthfully, 'An Afternoon's Outing'? Whatever it was, I decided, watching the children at their various activities or non-activities, it was, as Shakespeare said of sleep,

> *Balm of hurt minds . . .*
> *Chief nourisher in life's feast.*

We picked a few sprigs of downland vegetation and some twigs from the shrubs at the foot of the downs as we returned, as a sop to the Cerberus of education.

John Todd had collected a pocketful of rabbit droppings which he maintained were going to be used as fertiliser for his mum's pot-plants. My only proviso was that his collection should be put into a paper bag until home time. I heard him later telling another boy that he thought he might sell some to his granny.

Sometimes I think that John Todd will end up either in jail, or as a millionaire. He will certainly make his mark somewhere.

I relished returning to my Beech Green home on those golden afternoons of early term time. The gardening jobs which had waited during the rainy holidays were soon done, and Bob Willet came to lend a hand on Saturday mornings when he could spare the time.

'You heard about Mrs Mawne?' he asked, as we sat with our mugs of coffee in the sunshine.

'No. What's happened?'

'Been took to hospital. Lungs, they say.'

This was bad news. I liked Mrs Mawne, a strong-minded busy soul who took an active part in Fairacre affairs, and looked after her husband Henry very well. Henry was a well-known ornithologist and naturalist and wrote, not only for our *Caxley Chronicle*, but also for more erudite publications. At one time, when it was thought he was a bachelor, and before his wife returned to him, Fairacre had been busy arranging what it considered a suitable match between Henry and me. Naturally, neither of us knew anything about these romantic plans, and very cross we were when light dawned.

'Is it serious?'

'Must be if she's in hospital,' said Bob, who appeared to regard these institutions as the seemly place to die in. 'She do smoke, of course. Don't do your tubes any good.'

'And what about Mr Mawne? Can he look after himself?'

'Shouldn't think so,' said Bob cheerfully. 'Probably frizzle a hegg and bacon.'

'That's something, anyway.'

'Not as good as my Alice's steak and kidney pudden, or her rabbit pie with a nice bit of onion in it.'

'Well, you're spoilt,' I told him.

'That's right,' he agreed with much satisfaction.

He drained his mug and went back to his weeding.

During the next week, Henry Mawne appeared at school.

This was no surprise, as he is a frequent visitor bringing pamphlets and posters about birds and other natural matters which he thinks will interest the children. They always enjoy his visits, and sometimes he stays for half an hour and gives an impromptu nature lesson.

On this occasion I thought he looked older and shabbier. I enquired after his wife, and he shook his head sadly.

'Not too good. The medics tell me she had a slight stroke yesterday. Nothing to worry about, they tell me.' His face grew pink. 'I ask you! Nothing to worry about indeed! They told me not to visit her last night, but I'm damn well going up this afternoon.'

'I'm sure you'll find her getting on well,' I assured him,

hoping that was the truth. 'Lots of people have strokes, and are as right as rain soon after.'

He was not to be comforted, however, and took himself off after a few minutes. It was sad to see him suddenly so old.

'What's up?' I heard Patrick whisper to Ernest.

'Mrs Mawne. She's been struck.'

'Struck? By lightning or something?'

'No, chump! With a stroke, like that chap down the pub.'

'But he's all —' began Patrick looking horrified.

'That'll do,' I said firmly. 'You can stop talking and get on with your work.'

Resignedly, and with heavy sighs, they returned to their labours, while I sorted out a pile of forms to take home to study in peace before returning them to our local education office. Somehow, there seemed to be more than ever these days, and I did not relish an evening poring over them.

Henry's sad face haunted me. If his wife were laid up in hospital for any length of time it might be a good idea to have him to a meal one evening.

What Fairacre and Beech Green would make of the matter I did not know, nor care. If two middle-aged old dears could not enjoy a meal together without scandal it was a pity.

Nevertheless, I resolved to ask our vicar Gerald Partridge and his wife, or failing that, my old friends George and Isobel Annett to join the party. Decorum apart, four would fit nicely round my table, and make more cheerful company for a sad man.

Mrs Pringle, when she appeared at midday to wash up the dinner things, knew all about Mrs Mawne's troubles. With lugubrious relish she told me about several stroke sufferers of her acquaintance. None, it seemed, had survived, or if they had, she told me, it was a great pity considering the plight in which they were left.

'I don't want to hear anymore,' I told her roundly, and left her quivering with anger and frustration amidst the washing-up steam.

Later that evening I tried to settle down to those wretched forms, but found my attention wandering. Mrs Pringle's ghoulish enjoyment of disaster, which I can usually dismiss with some amusement, irritated me unduly on this particular evening. I had lived long enough with her, in all conscience, to be able to ignore her habitual gloom, but I had to admit that latterly she had riled me more than usual.

Was she getting even more trying, or was I getting crabbier? Of course, we were both getting older and our tempers became less equable. Even so, I thought, stuffing the forms into a file and abandoning the task for the moment, should I be feeling quite so depressed?

Perhaps I was sickening for something? Perhaps I needed more stimulus? Perhaps I needed company? Even Tibby seemed to have deserted me on this particular evening, going about some private feline business.

I walked out into the garden, still troubled. Heavy clouds had rolled up from the west, and no doubt rain would fall during the night. This was the first overcast evening we had seen for many days, and it fitted my mood. The air was still, somehow menacing, and I shivered despite the humid warmth.

I would go early to bed, I told myself, and read the latest Dick Francis book, and perhaps plan my proposed dinner party.

> *We get the Hump,*
> *Camelions Hump,*

as Rudyard Kipling said. Doing something was the cure for that, and tomorrow I should be myself again.

I was in bed by nine o'clock.

CHAPTER 2

Old and New Friends

The roads were wet when I set off for school the next morning, feeling rather more cheerful after my early night.

Mrs Pringle was limping heavily about her duties, and was decidedly off-hand with me. Mrs Pringle's bad leg is a sure pointer to prevailing conditions. If she is in one of her rare moods of comparatively good temper, she walks at her normal waddle.

If, however, the limp is noticeable, it means that she is resentful of all the work she is called upon to do, or she is in a flaming temper about one of her pet interests. Anything connected with the misuse of her precious tortoise stoves, for instance, puts her in a rage and the limp is most pronounced. When Mrs Pringle's leg has 'flared up', as she says, we are on guard.

Obviously, the present malaise was the outcome of my short shrift with her over Mrs Mawne's condition, and I did not propose to do any mollifying. She must just get on with it.

In my first months at Fairacre I had worried about Mrs Pringle's feelings, and had done my best to apologise for any hurt which I might have done her unknowingly. Now I knew better, and it was Bob Willet who had opened my eyes not long after my arrival.

'Don't you take no heed of that ol' besom's tantrums,' he told me sturdily. 'Maud Pringle's been a bad-tempered old bag ever since she was born. Turn a deaf ear and a blind eye.'

It was sound advice, and nowadays Mrs Pringle's temper and her bad leg's combustibility held no terrors for me.

Mrs Richards, my assistant, was on playground duty after we had finished school dinner, so I walked down to the Post Office to buy boiled sweets to replenish the school sweet tin, and to pay in some of the children's savings. This thrifty habit had started, years before my arrival, as a wartime effort, and somehow continued.

Mr Lamb greeted me with his usual *bonhomie* and his habitual crack about how many sweets I got through.

I asked after Mrs Mawne. Mr Lamb has his finger on the pulse of Fairacre life and knows more even than Mrs Pringle.

'Much the same, Mr Mawne told me. He's just been in for some eggs. Must be living on 'em, I reckon. They're keeping her in hospital for at least another week. He visits daily, afternoons mostly.'

Armed with this knowledge I decided to go ahead with my invitations that evening, and returned to my duties.

One of Fairacre's major interests at this time was the completion of the second new home which was to house five more children under the Trust's guardianship.

The first home was now flourishing, and the couple who ran it had settled happily among their neighbours. Their charges who had swelled my school's numbers were good-tempered easy children, and gave me no trouble.

The couple for the second home had been appointed, and were frequently seen watching last-minute alterations to their new house. The plumbing problem which had held up proceedings seemed to have been overcome, and it was generally expected that the family would arrive some time in October.

After school one day I walked over to make myself known to the man and woman who were working in the garden.

'We were going to call on you,' the man said. 'You'll be having our children I believe.'

'And very welcome they will be,' I told him.

We introduced ourselves. They were Molly and Alfred Cotton, and they already knew their neighbours and co-hosts the Bennetts from next door. They also knew Mr Lamb, Bob Willet and Jane and Tom Winter who lived close by.

The Winters' home was one of the three new houses to be built recently in the village, and Jane and Tom had moved in some time earlier. They were a friendly pair, and their young son Jeremy had made friends with the four newcomers as soon as they had settled in. The Cottons were delighted with their appointment as joint wardens to their five children, and it seemed pretty obvious to me that they would be a great asset to the village.

'You won't be having all our children,' Molly told me. 'The youngest is not walking yet, and the next up is only four. The two brothers, seven and nine, will come to you, and the girl who is ten.'

I said that I should welcome them, and asked a little more about their family.

'The two brothers and the baby are all from one family,' said Alfred. 'They were saved by neighbours from a fire at their home. The parents perished.'

'That's a terrible thing!'

'They're young enough to have half-forgotten it,' said Molly, 'but I think the older boy, Bobby, still gets nightmares about fire. It's one reason why they have been moved right away, to give them a fresh start.'

'Well, you are doing a fine job,' I told them.

'Not very well paid though,' added Alfred, in a semi-jocular way.

Much later I was to recall that rather odd remark.

My old home at Fairacre, the school house which stood only a stone's throw across the playground from Fairacre school, had been badly damaged by a storm a few years earlier.

Luckily, no one was hurt, and I had already removed to Dolly Clare's cottage at Beech Green.

The repairs took some time, but eventually it was restored and put on the market. To my delight two friends of mine had bought it, and now lived there with their baby.

Horace and Eve Umbleditch had met at the preparatory school where he taught and she had been the school secretary. They had adopted village life with enthusiasm, and were generally liked. Horace had been roped in by the vicar as a general help to Henry Mawne, who made himself responsible for the finances and general welfare of St Patrick's. Now that Henry was so much engaged with his wife's illness, Horace was being called upon to do more, which he undertook very cheerfully.

I called to see Eve and the baby one afternoon after school. Young Andrew was sitting in his pram, bouncing about with enormous energy and making a bleating noise which his fond mother told me was singing.

Eve was ironing, but seemed happy enough to stop and put on the kettle.

'Horace won't be in for some time. Rugger practice,' she told me.

'Do they start as young as that?'

'Well, they all rush about wherever the ball happens to be. You don't see much *passing* of any elegance and skill, but they have a rattling good puff about, and get fearfully dirty and hungry, and everyone's happy, so I suppose it does them good.'

She looked through the window at the pram. The bleating had stopped.

'He's dropped asleep,' she said. 'I always suspect sudden silence. It usually means he's found something to eat. He made quite a meal of his pram strap last week.'

We sipped our tea, and I looked about my old sitting-room with affection.

'Tell me,' said Eve, sounding worried. 'Do you *mind*?'

'Mind?'

'About us living here. In your house.'

'Good heavens, no! Why should I? It looks lovely to me. And it isn't my house now. It was only *lent* to me, so to speak, while I taught at Fairacre school, just as it was lent to my predecessors.'

She looked relieved.

'I still can't believe it is our house. Well, *will* be when the mortgage is paid,' she added with a smile. 'I still feel that it belongs to you.'

'I promise not to haunt you,' I said, 'but I know how you feel. The ghosts of the Hopes, who taught here years ago, always seemed to be about, largely I think through Mrs Pringle's constant reminders of how *clean* Mrs Hope had kept the place, in contrast to my own sketchy house-keeping. I gather from Mrs P. that Mrs Hope dusted the tops of her doors daily, and any visitors had to brush their clothes and take off their shoes before entering.'

'I don't believe it.'

'Frankly, neither do I, but you know Mrs Pringle! She

has a way of telling you the most outrageous things, with such concentrated venom that one begins to think they are true.'

'Well, we're happy as sand-boys here, and I hope that all these other newcomers will settle in as contentedly as we have.'

She went on to tell me that she had made friends with Jane and Tom Winter and the Bennetts who were the foster-parents near by, but had not yet met the Cottons.

She asked after Mrs Mawne whom she knew, and with all this exchange of news about old and new friends it was six o'clock before I realised it.

'Tibby will be pretty off-hand with me,' I told Eve, as I hurried to my car.

'And Horace will with me,' she replied, 'if I don't get our dinner in the oven.'

We departed to cope with our respective tyrants.

Plans for my modest dinner party went ahead.

The Reverend Gerald Partridge and his wife would be away for a week visiting friends in Norfolk, but Isobel and George Annett, who lived near me at the school house in Beech Green, said that they would love to come.

They and Henry Mawne were invited for the next Wednesday evening when the house would be at its cleanest after Mrs Pringle's ministrations in the afternoon.

Now what should I give them? was the next problem. Cold salmon and salad would be elegant, and easily prepared, but already the evenings were getting an autumnal feel about them, and hot food is somehow more welcoming.

I put my load of school forms, records, files and general correspondence to one side – yet again – and let my thoughts dwell much more pleasurably on my entertaining.

Something that would look after itself in a casserole, I decided. Who wants their hostess in the kitchen at the last minute stirring sauce?

I thought of lamb cutlets, pork chops, steak and kidney. Perhaps rather heavy as an evening meal for four middle-aged people, I decided.

A brace of pheasants, a present from the farmer Mr Roberts after his final shoot of the season, still lay in the freezer. But pheasant can be surprisingly tough, and not everyone likes it. What about fish? A halibut steak apiece, in a good white sauce, would suit me well, but did my guests like fish?

In the end, I took the safe and rather mundane way out by settling for chicken, jointed neatly by the butcher for my proposed casserole, and served with seasonal vegetables supplied by Mr Willet from his garden.

I would make an apple and blackberry pie, and a raspberry mousse for dessert, and nice easy accommodating melon for starters. I had some fresh coffee beans, and if I could remember to buy some chocolate mints I should be well set up.

Having settled this in my own mind, I picked up the armful of school papers, thought better of it, put them all back, and watched a television programme until it was time for bed.

I found that I was ready for bed much earlier these days, and when I had time to think about it I felt vaguely worried by my increasing tiredness.

It was still a pleasure to see friends, to write to those at a distance, or to talk to them by telephone. I had real joy in planning such simple entertaining as my little dinner party. Even a jaunt to Caxley at the weekends held a certain excitement.

But, I had to admit that school these days was increasingly demanding. The actual teaching, and the company of the children, I still enjoyed. The fact that the fear of closure, because of dwindling numbers, had now receded, thanks to the advent of the two new homes provided by the Trust, was an enormous relief, and by rights I should be feeling on top of the world.

But I was not. There was nothing physically wrong with me, no sinister pains or lumps in evidence. It was just that somehow the sparkle seemed to have gone out of life.

From school life anyway, I told myself. I remembered Eve Umbleditch's anxiety about my relinquishment of the school house which had been my home for so many years. Could I, subconsciously, be missing it? I did not think so. I was blissfully content with Dolly Clare's cottage at Beech Green.

Certainly, my routine had been slightly altered. I needed to get up earlier and to make sure that the car was ready for its daily short drive.

But I had always woken early, and was at my liveliest in the morning hours, so that nothing could account for my present malaise. Of course, I was getting older, and expected to be slower, but I was beginning to feel worried by the mound of paperwork which seemed to accompany me everywhere.

Like most people, I had never taken kindly to form-filling, but when I looked back to my early years at Fairacre, it seemed to me that I used to dash them off, send them back to the education office, and forget the whole affair. Now each morning brought a pile of work, usually marked 'Urgent', and I was beginning to feel submerged and desperate.

I told myself sternly that most people had the same problems and one must just soldier on. With any luck, I should adjust to my load, just like a tired old cart-horse.

It was on one of these evenings when I was being firm with myself, and trying to whip up enough energy to tackle at least some of my papers, that my old friend Amy rang.

We first met at college many years ago. She was, and still is, pretty, vivacious and intelligent. She gave up work when she married James after only two years' teaching, but occasionally took on a short spell as a supply teacher in local schools, 'to keep my hand in', as she puts it. Occasionally, she has helped me at Fairacre school, and she has certainly not lost her touch.

Our friendship has stood the test of time remarkably well, despite our different circumstances. Amy is much more sophisticated than I am, is a wonderful wife to James, and a wonderful hostess to the important business friends they entertain. She dresses exquisitely, keeps up-to-date with the world of music, theatre, films and painting, and generally puts me in the shade, where I am very content to stay.

The one really trying trait in Amy's character is her desire to see me married, and I have lost count of the various men she has paraded before me in her quest to find me a suitable partner. I am loud and vehement in my protestations to dear Amy, but it does no good. She cannot believe that any woman can be happy without a man in the house.

I constantly point out that I should find a husband a nuisance. I do not want to wash socks, thread new pyjama cords through hems with a safety-pin, listen to news of rugby teams, the stock market, golf averages and, in the case of older men, their war-time reminiscences. Besides, even the nicest men snore, and I like a peaceful bedroom.

Luckily, on this occasion, husbands were not on Amy's mind.

'It's about the opera,' said Amy, after our usual enquiries after health. 'There's a good company coming to Oxford. Care to join me one evening? James will be in China on some trade lark.'

'What's on offer?' I am no opera fan. The idiocy of the plots I find infuriating, and I don't know enough about music to appreciate the finer points. In any case, I have exceptionally acute hearing, and find the noise excessive. Before now I have sat through an entire opera with cotton wool in my ears, to the disgust of the opera-lovers around me. Even so, I have returned home with a splitting headache.

'They're only doing two,' replied Amy. '*Madame Butterfly* and *Die Fledermaus*.'

'Which do you favour?'

'Well, I like Puccini's music, but I like *Fledermaus* because it's such a romp. I want you to choose.'

'I do draw the line at *Madame Butterfly* because the plot's even more silly than most, and I can't stick Lieutenant Pinkerton, nor that ghastly inevitable toddler who turns up, and Butterfly is such a *wimp* —'

'Say no more,' said Amy, 'I gather you don't like it. So *Fledermaus* it is.'

I felt suddenly guilty.

'But Amy, if you prefer —'

'I'd rather see the Strauss one, actually. I love Frosch, the jailer, and all his bits of business.'

'You're sure?'

'Positive. I'll send off for the tickets today. It's not until early December. Make a note of the day now, my dear, as I expect you'll be up to your ears in end-of-term jollities by then.'

I told her about my dinner-party plans, and about poor disconsolate Henry Mawne.

'Well,' said Amy briskly, 'your company should cheer him up. He was always so fond of you.'

She hung up before I could protest.

There was a nip in the air as I drove to school the next morning. Already the swallows were gathering on the telephone lines ready for departure to sunnier places. The rose hips glowed like scarlet beads in the hedges, and the first few puffs of wild clematis seed-heads were a foretaste of the grey clouds which would soon obscure the bushes over which they clambered.

Autumn in this part of the world is always lovely, for we are blest with magnificent clumps of beech trees which thrive in this chalk country, and their blazing bronze lights the landscape when the sun shines upon them. I relish, too, the fruits of the earth, the blackberries, the crab apples, the sloes, and most of all the miraculous mushrooms, overnight pearls, which are a source of constant pleasure to those who come across them.

I am ready, too, for the domestic pleasures of colder days.

There is great satisfaction from the open fire in the cool evenings, particularly if it is fed with wood gathered by oneself. With the curtains drawn against the dark outside world, what could be more snug?

And yet I am sad too at the onset of winter. I miss the flowers, the smell of cut grass, the singing birds, the humming bees, and all the scents and sounds of summer. The smell of autumn bonfires, the departure of the swallows, the bare brown fields and the basket full of blackberries are small consolation for that golden summer sun.

When I arrived at school that morning, a little knot of children had gathered round a ladder on which Bob Willet was perched.

He was replacing a tile which had slipped a foot or two from its rightful place, and had lodged in the gutter.

'Been meaning to do this since the summer holidays,' he called down. 'You got enough rain through that dratted skylight without another leak here.'

I agreed. Our school is over a hundred years old and needs constant vigilance to keep it weatherproof. Under Bob Willet's care we are kept warm and dry. The skylight, though, has defied generations of builders, and leaks when-ever the wind and rain come from the south-west, its usual quarter.

He gave a final tap to the tile and began to descend the ladder. The performance over, the children began to look about for different excitements.

'Miss, miss,' called one of the new children who lived in the Bennetts' house. 'May I ring the bell?'

So far, the child had been very quiet, a pretty pale girl but shy. To offer to ring the bell was a great advance.

'I ain't rung it for *ages*!' growled Joseph Coggs. I have a soft spot for Joe, whose home and family are poor and pathetic, mainly because Arthur Coggs, the father, is incapa-ble of keeping a job and lives mostly in the local public houses.

'You often ring it,' I pointed out. 'But Alice has never done it. You can go inside with her, and get the bell rope down for her.'

'But can I ring it?'

'No. Perhaps just *once* to show her, and then it's Alice's job.'

Beaming, the two departed, and the rest drifted away to savour their last few minutes of freedom.

'I hear you're having Mr Mawne to supper this week,' said Bob. He was lowering the ladder carefully.

The way that news flies around a village never ceases to dumbfound me.

'Yes,' I said shortly.

'That's nice of you,' commented Bob. 'Poor old boy looks pretty glum these days.'

I did not answer, but began making my way to the school porch.

Bob Willet straightened up, red in the face from his exertions.

'There's a lot in Fairacre says you're a tough old biddy, but I allus maintain your 'eart's in the right place.'

He trudged off, leaving me speechless at Fairacre's assessment of my character.

Tough old biddy indeed!

CHAPTER 3

A Broken Evening

Mrs Pringle, of course, knew about my proposed evening party almost as soon as I did.

I do not think she approved of my invitation to Henry Mawne. She probably thought me *fast*, and possibly *loose*.

But she was graciously pleased to approve of my inclusion of the Annetts in the invitation. She knows both well. Isobel, in her single days, was my valued assistant after Dolly Clare's retirement, and her neat ways were much approved by Mrs Pringle.

'Leaves the classroom a fair treat,' was her summing up, and praise could go no higher.

George Annett has been organist and choir master at St Patrick's for many years, and has put up with Maud Pringle's contralto bellowings, not unlike a cow deprived of its calf, for all that time. By nature a quick and impatient man, he certainly finds Mrs Pringle a sore trial in the choir.

Her singing is powerful but not accurate. She tends to be slightly behind the rest of the choir in time, and decidedly flat when it comes to high notes.

Nevertheless, she is a faithful member of the choir, and takes a proprietorial interest in the chancel woodwork, particularly the choir stalls, as a forebear of hers was one of the carpenters and joiners who refurbished that area during Victoria's reign.

She approved of my having the party on a Wednesday evening.

'Give me a chance to do you properly on Wednesday afternoon,' she said. 'Leave out that cutlery of yours and I'll give it a good go, and get the egg out of the forks.'

I said that I should be grateful for such help.

'Of course, the windows really wants cleaning, and that carpet's never been the same since you tripped over with the cheese sauce in your hand. And to my mind, that fireplace always looks *tawdry*. Never comes up like my stoves here.'

'Well, you can't expect it. The stoves get attention every day.'

'That's true,' agreed Mrs Pringle with smug satisfaction. 'I takes a pride in 'em. I suppose if your head's full of book-learning it hasn't got enough go left in it to notice the filth around the place.'

Whether this was a compliment to my intelligence, or a real back-hander to my domestic standards, I could not be sure. A bit of both, I thought, and decided to let it pass without comment.

In any case, Mrs Pringle likes to have the last word.

On the evening of the party everything looked splendid.

The table was spread with my best tablecloth, which had been left to me by Aunt Clara, together with her seed pearls and a very welcome hundred pounds, some thirty years ago. The glass and silver sparkled, and a vase of late roses stood in the centre of the table.

I felt that my ancient place mats rather let the side down, but they were pretty on top, if shabby, and no one was likely to turn them over to examine the deplorable state of the baize backing during a polite dinner party.

The evening was chilly, and I thought of my chicken

casserole simmering away in the oven with some satisfaction. Perhaps I should have had soup for starters instead of melon? Too late now, I told myself, and went upstairs to change.

Through the bedroom window I could just see, as the dusk deepened, that the Bramley apples were almost ready to pick, and a few autumn leaves were strewn on the lawn. Mrs Pringle had set a fire for us, and it was now crackling away, throwing cheerful flickers of rosy light on the walls of my sitting-room, and glinting on the newly polished copper and brass.

The Annetts were the first to arrive. Isobel was in a pretty dove-grey knitted suit and a handsome silk blouse, and George very spruce in his Sunday suit and a dashing Liberty tie.

'My!' he exclaimed, warming his hands at the fire. 'You have made it all look so splendid! Dolly would be so pleased to see it.'

'I wish she could,' I replied. 'I only hope I can care for it as well as she did.'

Henry drove up a few minutes later. He looked a little less strained, I thought, as we asked for the latest bulletin on his wife's condition.

'A little better, they said, when I rang just now. But no hope of her returning home, evidently, until all the tests are favourable.'

We all agreed that it was far better to stay a little longer in the nurses' care, and to get really strong before facing the rigours of home affairs.

'Have you met our newcomer yet?' asked George. 'You'd be interested in him, Henry. He has written a book about birds of prey.'

'Not old Jenkins?' said Henry.

'That's right.'

'We were up at Cambridge together. Never kept in

touch though. Where is he? He married some frightful woman in Kenya.'

'Well, she died out there, and he's returned home. He's taken that little house just off the road between here and Fairacre. Up Pig Lane.'

'It's called Downland Lane now,' I pointed out. 'Some of the new people thought Pig Lane was vulgar.'

'I still call it Pig Lane,' said Henry.

'So do I,' said George roundly.

'I'll look him up,' promised Henry. 'I read his book. Not bad at all, considering Jenkins wrote it.'

I left them to it while I went to dish up.

I must say that my guests were most appreciative, and I basked in the warmth of their compliments. I am told that in some circles it is not considered polite to comment on the food served, but in these parts we take an active interest in the food put before us, and have no inhibitions about expressing our pleasure. I was grateful for my visitors' enthusiasm and pleased to see their hearty appetites.

The conversation flowed easily. The newcomer was described by Henry, as he remembered him at university, as 'a decent sort of fellow, but a bit of a dreamer'.

George Annett wanted to know if he could sing. Both the Fairacre and Beech Green church choirs were in need of male voices.

This led to next spring's Caxley Festival, then a concert the Annetts had been to in London, and on to more homely affairs such as the imminent glut of apples, the failure of our local runner beans, and the good fortune of Fairacre school in having found eight or nine new pupils to stave off the possibility of closure.

We adjourned to the fireside again, and I served coffee and passed round the box of mints which I had managed to remember.

It was while we were thus happily engaged that the telephone rang and I went to answer it.

A woman, sounding rather weary, spoke to me.

'This is the County Hospital. We are trying to get in touch with Mr Mawne – Mr Henry Mawne – and have been told that he is staying with you.'

I was somewhat taken aback by this suggestion that Henry was a resident in my home, but replied that Henry Mawne was here at the moment and that I would fetch him.

I returned to my friends feeling extremely worried. It must be serious news if the hospital were urgently seeking Henry.

They stopped their conversation as I entered, and looked up, coffee cups suspended.

'It's the hospital, Henry,' I said gently.

Henry struggled to his feet, the colour draining from his face.

I led him through to the telephone, and made him sit down before handing him the receiver, and then returned to the Annetts. They looked as shaken as I felt.

'It must be his wife,' whispered Isobel. 'But she was getting on so well. He said that he rang before coming here.'

The happiness of the evening was suddenly shattered by this interruption. I refilled coffee cups, and went about my duties as a hostess with a very sick feeling.

Henry reappeared after a few minutes. His face was ashen.

'I must go at once,' he muttered. 'She's conscious, asking for me. The sister said something about a rapid deterioration.'

He looked so shaky that I hastened towards him to propel him to a chair, but he motioned me away distractedly.

'I'm so sorry, but I must go at once. Thank goodness I've got the car outside.'

'Let me give you some more coffee before you go,' I urged, but he would have none of it.

'I must hurry. I intended to give the hospital this number before I left home, but forgot. Luckily, Bob Willet was potting up in my conservatory and got their message. But, of course, he had to look up this number, and there was some delay. It's urgent that I set off.'

George stood up. 'I shall drive you,' he said firmly.

Poor Henry's face crumpled, and for a moment I thought that he would break down. But he took a deep breath, thanked me very touchingly for the evening, and went with George to the car.

'But how will you get back,' whispered Isobel, 'if Henry stays?'

'There are always taxis,' said George, following his passenger, who was now opening the car door. 'Stay here until I ring from the hospital.'

We went to see them off, sending all sorts of hopeful messages to the invalid, but with heavy hearts.

'Heaven help all three of them,' I said to Isobel, when we were back by the fire. I held up the coffee pot.

'I couldn't, thanks. Let's wash up.'

'No, no!' I protested, but was overborne.

'Please. We won't do any good moping here. Let's mope while we do the dishes and wait for George to ring.'

And so we did.

It is some twenty miles to our County Hospital, and it was over an hour before George rang to say that he was returning by taxi. Henry was staying overnight and his car had been left in the hospital car park.

'And his wife?'

'Touch and go, I gather, but she spoke to Henry, which comforted him greatly.'

'I'm glad you drove him,' I said. 'He was in no state to be in charge of a car.'

'I'll be with you in half an hour,' he promised, as I handed the receiver to Isobel.

He kept his word, and we all had the final drink of the evening before the two set out to walk home.

The stars were out, and the night was still and chilly. I returned from my gate breathing in the unmistakable scent of autumn.

On the whole, I thought, as I put down on the kitchen floor some delectable remains of the chicken for Tibby, it had been a happy evening. But what a sad ending!

And what would the morrow hold for poor Henry?

The next morning Bob Willet met me in the school playground in a most unusual state of agitation.

'I've been that worried ever since the hospital called,' he told me. 'I didn't want to give 'em your number and upset the party, but they was so pushy – kept on and on – and in the end I thought I'd do as they said. I do hope that was right.'

'Absolutely,' I told him, and went on to explain the urgency of the matter and that Mr Mawne was staying with his wife.

He seemed much relieved. 'That's a comfort to me. If there's one thing I hates it's a Meddlesome Mattie, and I couldn't sleep last night for wondering if I'd done the right thing.'

'You did. And your vegetables were much appreciated.'

'And my brights?' boomed Mrs Pringle, who had appeared in time to hear the end of our conversation.

'They made the place look like Buckingham Palace,' I assured her.

With comparative peace restored we all three returned to our daily round.

Amy came to see me that evening, bearing a large suitcase filled with cast-off clothes and household linen, for an imminent school jumble sale.

'Good heavens, Amy!' I exclaimed, turning over some elegant jumpers and skirts. 'I think I shall take first pick.'

'Not your colours, dear,' replied Amy, settling herself on the sofa. 'Besides, it's quite wrong to snaffle all the best things before the sale starts. It's done far too often at Bent and elsewhere, but I hoped that Fairacre had more moral integrity.'

'My, my, Amy! You make me feel like an opium-runner or white-slaver! In any case, we have an admirable practice in Fairacre when it comes to jumble sales and bazaars.'

'And what's that?'

'The helpers are allowed to pick one object – and one only – before the doors open. After all, they've done the donkey work, and it does seem to work well.'

'I shall introduce the practice at Bent,' promised Amy. 'Now tell me how the party went.'

I told her all. She shook her head sadly.

'Poor woman! One wonders if it would be kinder to see her go if things are as bad as that. Poor Henry, too: he will be lonely.'

She looked at me with the speculative gaze I have learnt to dread.

'Like a cup of coffee?' I asked hastily.

'Love one. And by the way, James sent a message to say that your second house will definitely be ready at half term.'

Amy's husband was one of the directors of the Malory-Hope Trust, and his particular part in its work was the seeking of suitable family-sized houses for the orphans in the care of the Trust. He had recently been instrumental in buying some terraced houses in Glasgow for this work, and since then the two new Fairacre houses which had remained empty for so long.

I had wondered if James had thought of the possible closure of my school when the Trust had purchased this new property, and I had certainly felt somewhat guilty about the school's dwindling pupils.

When I taxed James with my guilty fears, he was hot in denying it. The fact was, he told me, that the property was never going to be as cheap again, so that he knew he would be getting a bargain on the Trust's behalf. Secondly, Sir Derek Malory-Hope, the original founder, had been keen to have several local homes and had expressed this wish a short time before his death. James, as his friend and colleague, was simply carrying out his desires.

I accepted this explanation absolutely, but I was aware that the decision to buy the two houses had been a life-saver for the school I had cared for so long. We were all much indebted to the Malory-Hope Trust.

Amy and I sipped our coffee, and I was conscious that she was watching me closely.

'You look rather tired,' she said. 'That dinner party must have worn you out.'

'Not the party,' I told her, 'but I must admit that the news from the hospital shook us all.'

'It must have done. But James and I have thought you've seemed under the weather for some time. Are you overworking?'

'Me? Overworking?' I cried. 'Amy, you've known me long enough to know that I have an in-built laziness that makes sure that I don't strain myself.'

'Well, I know you *procrastinate*, and you *dither*. Look at the dozens of jobs you've thought about over the years and never applied for. And here you are, wasted and washed up, still at Fairacre.'

'Thank you for those few kind words. You make me feel like a dish cloth.'

Amy laughed, and patted my arm. 'No offence meant, and none taken I hope, but seriously, you do look a little *wan*. What about having a check-up with the doctor?'

'I'm not bothering him. He's quite enough to do with people who are really ill.'

'Then take a tonic. An iron tonic might be just the thing.'

'The sort you take through a straw so that your teeth don't go black? I haven't done that since I was about six.'

Amy snorted impatiently. 'No, no! They have *pills* these days. Sometimes I wonder where you have been all these years.'

'Here,' I said cheerfully. 'And here, Amy dear, I propose to remain.'

'Hopeless!' sighed Amy.

I studied my face in the looking-glass when I went to bed. As far as I could see, I looked much the same. Older, of course, hair greying, jaw-line definitely heavier, plenty of lines here and there, but I was still recognisable, I thought.

It was nice of Amy to worry over me, but unnecessary. I certainly felt tired, and once or twice had been slightly dizzy, as when the vicar had told me about the new pupils who would be attending Fairacre school. And, of course, I was reluctant to get up in the mornings, but with autumn beginning to cast its chill across the country this was understandable. As for consulting our hard-pressed doctor, the idea was simply ludicrous, I told my reflection sternly.

Two days passed with no real news about Henry Mawne's wife, who remained critically ill in hospital.

Henry was at home, staying within earshot of the telephone, and with his car ready to set off if a call came.

We all worried about him, and even Mrs Pringle seemed genuinely sympathetic, curbing her usually ghoulish comments and simply shaking her head when Bob Willet mentioned the invalid.

But one evening Gerald Partridge rang me. Our vicar's voice was shaking.

'I heard about midday,' he told me. 'She died without regaining consciousness, and I've been with Henry. He's taken it very quietly and bravely. I think he knew all along that it was hopeless. I grieve for the poor fellow.'

I asked about funeral arrangements.

'Family only at the county crematorium. No flowers or letters, as she directed. And the remains will go to the family plot in Ireland. A melancholy journey for Henry. I have offered to go with him.'

It was a short conversation and I put the receiver down feeling very sad.

Another link with Fairacre life was broken.

Half term came at the end of October, and I spent most of it in the company of my cousin Ruth who lives in Dorset.

Her parting words were, 'You look better than when you arrived,' which I found faintly disquieting. How dilapidated had I looked on arrival, I wondered?

I returned to find four Christmas catalogues, as well as the usual letters.

Could Christmas really be so imminent? Visions of carols to be learnt, a nativity play, the usual Fairacre school party given to friends in the village, paper chains, Christmas cards and calendars to be constructed, all passed before my inward eye, and I thought, like Wordsworth, of the bliss of solitude.

Ah well! I had done it before, I comforted myself, and no doubt I could cope with it again.

Mrs Pringle greeted me with the news that the Cottons' house was now in order, and that the children would be coming to school, probably that very morning.

I viewed the prospect with pleasure, and hoped that they would settle with us as happily as their next-door neighbours, the Bennett children, had done.

Sure enough, as Joseph Coggs pulled the school bell rope, a blissful smile lighting up his gipsy-dark face, Mrs Cotton arrived with three of the five children.

There was a fair-haired girl of about ten, and two brothers of seven and nine. These two, I knew, were the children who had lost their parents in a fire. A younger child, not related to the brothers, would be eligible for

admission next term when she would have her fifth birthday. An even younger girl, sister to the two brothers, was
still only a toddler, and it would be some time before I had
the pleasure of entering her name in the school register.

All the three newcomers came into my class. There was
a certain amount of staring and whispering among my old
hands, but within half an hour the three had settled in, and
there was a general atmosphere of acceptance from new
and old pupils.

The brothers seemed to be exceptionally well advanced
in their school work. They had been attending a school in
a neighbouring county, and I began to wonder if my
teaching methods were behind the times. Were these two
unusually forward, or were my children less intelligent?
Was I falling down in my duties? Perhaps I should go to
those refresher courses always being urged upon me by the
school authorities. Too often such missives ended up on
the wastepaper pile, together with all those harrowing
appeals to save deprived people, starving children, diminish-
ing rain forests, endangered species and sufferers from a
multitude of agonising diseases.

I am far from callous, and frequently have a few sleepless
hours at night worrying about these horrors which come
tumbling through the letter-box. But there is a limit to my
ability to help, and I simply support four or five pet
charities, and have done so faithfully over the years.

Perhaps those pamphlets about evening classes and weekend refresher courses should be rescued from the pile, and
studied earnestly?

Certainly my three newcomers seemed to be well in
advance of Fairacre's standards in reading, writing and arith-
metic.

I was filled with misgivings.

*

Our vicar usually takes prayers at the school one day a week, but a message came to say that he was accompanying Henry Mawne to Ireland for the interment of his wife's ashes, and would not be able to come to the school as usual.

Mrs Pringle seemed to take this news as a personal affront.

'Poor Mr Partridge, having to go all that way for a burial! If Mrs Mawne had been laid to rest decently in Fairacre churchyard, he could have come to school like he always does, and I could have got my stoves polished just as usual.'

I enquired why the vicar's visits should upset the stoves' routine.

'They always gets a special blackleading before vicar's day,' she told me. 'Surely you've noticed?'

I had to admit that I had not. Her breathing became heavier than usual, and her face turned red with outrage.

'Sometimes I wonders,' she puffed, 'why I spend my time working my fingers to the bone in this place, day after day, week after week —'

She paused for breath.

'Year after year,' I prompted helpfully.

'Pah!' said Mrs Pringle, and limped away.

That combustible leg of hers would register disgust, I knew, for the rest of the day.

CHAPTER 4

Personal Shock

Henry Mawne was in Ireland for three weeks, staying with his wife's relations.

During that time he sent me a sad little note thanking me for the evening he had shared at my house with the Annetts. He described it as 'a warm and comforting spot in a bleak world', but felt that he was slowly getting back to normal after the distress of the past weeks.

The vicar was only away for two nights, returning immediately after the service in which he had taken part.

He told me something about it when he called just after school closed one wet afternoon.

I was unlocking my car when he arrived, the children and Mrs Richards having departed.

I went to greet him, and made tracks for the school door, but he waved me back to the car, and we sat side by side watching the splashing of raindrops into the play-ground puddles.

'I found the occasion very moving,' he said. 'Such a green and lovely spot. I think Henry might be persuaded to stay permanently. He met his wife there, you know, and her family are being very pressing.'

'Would it be a good thing? Is there anything to bring him back here?'

Gerald Partridge looked troubled. 'I hope he does decide

to stay here. He is such a tower of strength to me over church affairs, and he is very well-liked in the locality. Also he said that this drier climate suits him better,' he said, surveying the puddles.

'In any case,' I said, 'he will have to return to do something about the house, I imagine.'

We sat in silence for a few minutes, the rain drumming on the car roof, and the windscreen running with water.

'Henry said how much he had enjoyed his evening with you,' said the vicar. 'But he thought you looked rather tired.'

My heart sank. Did I really look such an old hag these days?

'You are well, I hope,' went on the vicar, turning in his seat to study me anxiously.

'I'm fine,' I said firmly. 'Right as a trivet, whatever that may mean.'

'Good, good! Can't have you under the weather, you know. It's a miserable time of year.'

'I'll run you back,' I said. 'The rain's getting heavier.'

We trundled through the gathering gloom of a November afternoon, and I dropped him at his front door, refusing his kind invitation to tea.

Driving under the dripping trees to Beech Green, I pondered on this recent display of concern for my health.

Maybe I should get an iron tonic, as Amy had suggested.

The thought was disquieting, but I put aside my health problems after tea, and bravely settled down to some of my growing pile of paper work.

I found it heavy going, and by seven o'clock I was beginning to wonder, yet again, if all these questionnaires and forms were really necessary.

While I was looking back to the relatively free-from-form days of yesteryear, in a nostalgic mood, Amy rang to enquire after my health.

'What about that iron tonic? Have you seen the doctor? Are you sleeping and eating properly?'

'Oh, Amy!' I cried. 'It's sweet of you to be so concerned about me, but I am perfectly healthy. Simply lazy, that's all.'

'Well, I don't believe that, and all I wanted to say was that I hope you will come for a weekend soon, and we can see that you get a proper rest and some food.'

I began to feel like a victim of some national catastrophe being rescued by the Red Cross from starvation, homelessness and disease.

'What are you doing now?' queried Amy.

'Filling in quite unnecessary forms which should have been at the office last week.'

'That's no good to you,' said Amy firmly. 'Put them away, have a tot of whisky and go to bed.'

'I don't like whisky.'

Amy tutted impatiently. 'Well, hot milk then. With perhaps a raw egg in it.'

'It would go down like frogs' spawn! I couldn't face it.'

'What a tiresome girl you are! Anyway, take things quietly, and do let us know if we can do anything. Think about a weekend here. Any weekend suits us, except the next one. I've Lucy Colgate coming for the night, and I don't suppose you want to meet her?'

'Definitely not,' I agreed. Lucy Colgate had been at college with Amy and me. Amy, being of a more kindly disposition, had kept in touch, but I had always found Lucy pretentious, self-centred and irritatingly affected. I found that a little of Lucy's company went a long way.

'But thank you, my dear, for thinking of me, and I'll look forward to a weekend at Bent with enormous pleasure.'

After promising to eat, sleep, take iron tablets, consult my doctor in the near future, put my feet up whenever possible, and to Keep in Touch, I put down the receiver and went to feed Tibby.

The next morning my alarm clock failed to go off, and I awoke twenty minutes later than usual to a dark wet day.

Hurrying to the bathroom I noticed a heaviness in one foot, and supposed that I had been sleeping with it trapped under me.

Stumbling about, getting dressed, I felt annoyed that my foot and leg were taking so long to return to normal. However, there was absolutely no pain, and by the time I had snatched a hasty breakfast of cornflakes and a cup of coffee, I had forgotten the discomfort. It would wear off, I told myself, when I found that I had a slight limp on my way to the garage.

I drove to school determined to ignore a certain numbness in my left foot when using the clutch. Time to worry when something hurt, I told myself, and before long was so immersed in my school duties that I really did forget the trouble with my foot.

Preparations for Christmas were already starting, and Mrs Richards and I had decided that it was a year or two since we had embarked upon a nativity play, and that this Christmas we would produce a real masterpiece.

We had a number of Eastern costumes and various other props in a large box. We also had three shepherds' crooks which were stored in the overcrowded map cupboard along with rolled-up aids to education with such outdated labels as 'The British Empire 1925' and 'Aids to Resuscitation 1940'.

The vicar was enthusiastic about this project and invited the school to perform in St Patrick's chancel one afternoon towards the end of term.

'I think we might even have a collection. I'm sure that lots of parents and friends of the school would like to contribute to the Roof Fund.'

On this particular afternoon Mrs Richards and I took the children across to the church for a preliminary assessment of this natural stage offered to us.

The church was unheated, and uncomfortably dark and dank. I sat with the older children in the cold hard pews whilst Mrs Richards was busy positioning her children around the imaginary crib in the chancel.

As well as the physical discomfort I felt remarkably tired, and could have nodded off if I had been alone. It seemed a long time before Mrs Richards had arranged her groupings to her satisfaction, and I was glad to stir myself to take her place with my own class.

In the gloom I stumbled on the chancel steps but saved myself from falling by grabbing a choir stall.

We went through this first tentative rehearsal of positioning and then decided that it was too cold to linger. On our way back, Bob Willet hailed me from the churchyard.

'All right to bring you up some keeping apples?' he called. 'Alice's sister's given us enough for an army, and I've got to come your way after tea.'

I said that would be fine, and we made our way back to school.

'You're limping,' said my assistant. 'What's wrong?'

I told her about my numbed foot.

'Surely it shouldn't be *numb* for hours!'

'Well, sometimes it *tingles*,' I assured her. 'It's nothing. It doesn't hurt.'

'I should see the doctor,' said Mrs Richards.

'I should see the doctor,' said Bob Willet, when we were sitting at the kitchen table later that day.

He had watched me pouring tea into two mugs, and commented on my shaking hand.

'It's nothing,' I said shortly. I was beginning to get rather cross with all this advice. First Amy, then Mrs Richards, and now Bob. 'The pot's heavy, that's all.'

'Well, I've seen you pouring tea for years, and never seen you wobblin' about like a half-set jelly afore.'

'Those apples,' I said, nodding towards the box he had brought, and keen to change the subject, 'are more than welcome. Will they keep all right in the garden shed?'

'Wrapped up in a half-sheet of newspaper,' said Bob, 'they'll be sound as a bell till after Christmas.'

He finished his tea, and I bade him farewell at the door. The rain still pattered down, the trees dripped and the ground was soggy.

I returned to the kitchen. Should I wrap the apples now, or get on with the children's personal records as requested by the office?

Frankly, I felt too tired to face either. I leafed through the *Radio Times*, and was offered 'Sex Slavery in Latin America', a modern play described as 'explicitly sensual', or a quiz game which I knew from experience plumbed the depths of banality, to the accompaniment of deafening applause from the captive audience.

I cast the magazine from me, and eyed Tibby, blissfully asleep in the armchair.

An excellent idea, I thought, and went upstairs to my own bed.

The rain had stopped when I awoke next morning, and I told myself that now all would be well after such a long and deep sleep.

My foot still hampered me, and I had to admit that I was wobbling 'like a half-set jelly' as Bob Willet so elegantly put it. Perhaps I really ought to visit the doctor? The prospect was depressing.

Not that I had anything against the young man who was one of several who had come after our well-beloved Dr Martin who had died, but I did not relish spending part of my evening in his company. At least, I thought hopefully, as I drove to school, it would mean postponing those wretched personal records that were beginning to haunt me.

The vicar came to take morning prayers, and said when he left that I looked rather tired and that he hoped that I was not over-doing it.

Mrs Richards insisted on pouring the hot water into our coffee mugs at playtime as she could see that I was 'not quite right yet'.

Mrs Pringle, arriving to wash up after school dinner, said that her aunt, although a strict teetotaller, had 'staggered about' just as I was doing, 'looking as drunk as a lord'.

Joseph Coggs, who kindly accompanied me to my car at home time, carrying yet another heavy file of papers, said that his gran 'walked just like that, all doddery-like'.

I decided that it was high time to visit the doctor.

There were only four of us in the waiting-room, the other three unknown to me. One had an appalling cold which needed noisy attention into dozens of tissues which she stuffed after use up the sleeve of her cardigan. I did not feel that this was very hygienic, especially as a wastepaper basket stood nearby. However, I thought charitably, the germs were being kept closer to her own vicinity by her present method of disposal.

The other two were obviously a married couple, passing magazines to each other, and occasionally speaking in a hushed tone as if in the presence of the dead.

I helped myself to a magazine which soon posed some problems for a respectable single woman.

Question: Was I worried about my present sex life?

My answer: Not in the least. But nice of you to ask.

Question: Was my doctor sympathetic to my sex problems?

My answer: No idea. In any case I should not be troubling him with such matters this evening.

I got up to change this magazine for an ancient *Homes and Gardens*, which surely should provide more acceptable reading matter, when the door opened and I was summoned into the presence.

I knew Dr Ferguson slightly, and he was pleasantly welcoming. I explained my symptoms in unmedical terms, and he listened attentively.

After some questioning about my family history, he took my blood pressure and pulse, listened to my chest with an ice-cold stethoscope, and then said, 'There's nothing to worry about. I think you have simply had a very mild stroke.'

'Nothing to worry about?' I squeaked in horror. 'A stroke?'

'Not if you are sensible. Lots of people have slight strokes. There is no pain usually, and after a day or two one is over it.'

'But suppose I get a *bad* stroke? What can I do to stop any sort of stroke?'

I must admit that I was feeling thoroughly shocked by his diagnosis. Me, a stroke? It was unthinkable!

'The first thing to do is to face this calmly. It is not serious. It is simply a warning. Your body is telling you to avoid any sort of strain, mental and emotional as well as physical.'

I thought of my daily encounters with Mrs Pringle, and reckoned that my emotional strain, in just that one quarter, must be excessive.

'You are in sound health, except for slightly high blood pressure. I'll give you some tablets for that. The only advice you need is something you know already. Rest as much as possible, keep to a sensible diet, and *don't worry*! Come and see me in a week's time.'

He scribbled a prescription, handed it over and I rose to go.

At the door I turned.

'You know I am a teacher. Am I likely to have the sort of stroke that would knock me out in front of the children?'

He looked at me soberly, considering my question seriously, and I liked him for that.

'It is not likely, but it cannot be ruled out entirely.'

'Thank you,' I said, and tottered out to my car.

I could not get to sleep that night.

I have been exceptionally fortunate in having good health, and rarely had to take time off from school. One takes such a happy condition for granted until some blow, like this one, makes one realise that the body gives way occasionally.

My last question to Dr Ferguson had been the outcome of my main worry. I remembered, with painful clarity, the scene in the infants' room so long ago when Dolly Clare had collapsed.

She had been smitten with a heart attack, and had fallen forward across her desk. Her white hair lay in a puddle of water from an overturned flower vase. Her lips were a frightening blue colour and her eyes were closed. Gathered round her were a dozen or so terrified children, some in tears, and it had taken me some time to collect my wits and hurry them to my own room while I attended to the patient.

The incident had shocked me deeply, and had never been forgotten. Now I was facing a similar problem.

Here I lay, in Dolly Clare's bedroom, wondering what to do. Had she felt as I did now, shaky and full of doubts?

Dr Martin had told me on that dreadful afternoon that she had suffered one or two earlier attacks but had refused to give in. Would the same thing happen to me? Should I collapse as she did in front of a class of horror-struck children?

And what sort of state should I be left in? I thought of several people who still suffered from the effects of a stroke. Some were speechless, some were immobile, some were mentally affected. Was that to be my future too?

I tossed and turned, trying to find some comfort. I reminded myself of the doctor's words. It was only a warning. My general health was sound. I simply had to take things gently.

But how on earth could I? Visions of all that paperwork, of the extra effort needed for our Christmas celebrations, of Mrs Pringle and her infuriating ways, floated before my sleepless eyes. It was interesting, I noted, that the children did not readily spring to mind as an irritant, only as a vulnerable element to be protected.

At four o'clock I descended to the kitchen and made a pot of tea. Sitting there drinking, with a bleary-eyed Tibby hoping for an early morning snack, I began to think seriously about taking early retirement. I had just over two years to do. Should I be able to hang on? Was I truly fit enough to teach properly?

I remembered my surprise at the high level of ability shown by some of the new pupils. Were they naturally more intelligent or had they been better taught? It was a dispiriting thought.

Much troubled, I limped back to bed and fell into a few hours of exhausted slumber.

Of course, by the time I drove over to Fairacre, everything seemed brighter. The fears of the night, like a flock of malevolent vultures, had flown away, and I was sure that the doctor's words were true.

I had been given a warning, and that was all. If I did as he advised and took things sensibly, there was no reason why I should not continue at Fairacre school until my allotted time was up.

My foot seemed much better, and I entered the lobby in a buoyant mood.

Mrs Pringle was cleaning the wash basins, but turned to confront me, Vim tin in hand.

'I can see you've had a poor night of it,' she announced with ghoulish satisfaction. 'I was told you'd been to see the doctor. Bad news?'

'He said that I was in good health,' I snapped. I suddenly wished that he could be present to see just what I had to face every morning.

Mrs Pringle's expression was expectant. I knew that she was hoping for an account of everything that had passed between the doctor and me. I was determined not to fuel the fire, and strode with great dignity towards my class-room.

It was unfortunate that I tripped over the mat. Mrs Pringle gave a gasp which could have meant 'I told you so', as unharmed, but very cross, I went to my desk.

School affairs went on as usual for the next week or two, and gradually I began to get over my shock.

I remembered to take the prescribed tablets now and again, and went to bed earlier than usual, and duly visited the doctor as requested.

He seemed quite pleased with me, and spent a few of his precious minutes talking generally about my way of life.

Did I ever feel lonely, he asked me? Could I get domestic help easily? Did I have bouts of depression? He had found that some women of about my age were unhappy at times, probably because they were past child-bearing.

I must admit that this appeared an extremely odd remark to make to me. He was obviously a kindly and sympathetic man, and I recalled the somewhat impertinent personal questions posed in that women's magazine out in the waiting-room. But surely most married women of my age would have had what family they wanted – or did not want – and were quite looking forward to an easier time now that their children were off their hands.

'Of course,' he went on hurriedly, before I had time to comment, 'you don't have quite the same anxieties, as a single woman.'

'I rather think,' I told him, 'that most women, whether single or married, look forward to a sprightly middle age.'

'Well, I'm certain you will have one,' he assured me, as he ushered me out. 'There's no need for you to come again unless anything worries you.'

I sang all the way home.

CHAPTER 5

End of Term

The relief at my return to normal health gave a great lift to my spirits.

Suddenly I was inspired to tackle all kinds of jobs I had been postponing for weeks.

The dreaded paperwork began to diminish after several evenings of concentration, and I took part in the Christmas preparations with renewed vigour.

Thoroughly frightened at the thought that I might be smitten again, I took care to go to bed earlier than usual and to take my tablets regularly. I admit that I had been terribly scared.

I told no one about my stroke, but did tell kind enquirers that I had slightly high blood pressure which was responding to the prescribed tablets.

Over the years I have discovered that it is as well to provide something for curious minds to pore over. A flat denial of everything only whets the appetite of gossip-seekers. A judicious amount of truthful fact, willingly handed out, is enough to protect the main issue from being revealed.

Sounding disappointed, Mrs Pringle grudgingly admitted that I was 'looking quite bonny again'. Bob Willet said he was glad to see me 'picking up', and Mrs Richards said how good it was to see me as I 'used to be'.

It was early in December when the Annetts invited me

to supper to meet the Beech Green newcomer John Jenkins, the friend of Henry Mawne.

Henry too had been invited and picked me up on his way from Fairacre. He seemed to have settled back into his usual routine, and had acquired a housekeeper after whom I enquired as we drove the short distance to the school house where the Annetts lived.

'A bit bossy,' said Henry. 'I have to leave my shoes in the porch, and she will keep giving me onion sauce with everything. Still, she keeps the house very clean, and her cooking's passable. Nothing like as good as yours though.'

I felt gratified, although I doubted secretly if my efforts were any better than the housekeeper's.

Henry and John had already renewed their friendship, but this was the first time I had met John. He was a handsome man, tall and thin, with a mane of silvery hair and very bright blue eyes.

He looked ten years younger than the plump and bald Henry, but of course, I thought charitably, he has probably not had poor Henry's recent unhappiness.

It was a cheerful party, and as Isobel is an excellent cook we tucked into delicious food and drink. George Annett was in great form and was doing his best to persuade both men to join the choirs of their respective parish churches. He did not have much luck.

And then he turned to me and said something quite surprising.

'I hear you are thinking of retiring.'

I was considerably taken aback. My secret fears had been communicated to absolutely no one. What is there about country air which seems to dispense one's best-kept secrets to all and sundry?

'I have over two years to go until I'm of retiring age,' I managed to say.

'Oh! I somehow thought you had early retirement in mind. I'm soldiering on until sixty-five if my health allows. I must admit I'd like to go at sixty, but we can do with my salary for a little longer.'

'Retirement's really hard work,' observed John Jenkins. 'Everyone wants me to join something.'

'Like the choir?' said George.

John laughed, and Henry added, 'Well, I've been far busier as a so-called retired man than ever I was in business. Still, I do manage to enjoy my bird work, and that reminds me.'

He began to fumble in the breast pocket of his jacket, and brought out a leaflet.

'I'm giving a little talk with slides in Caxley early in the New Year. Would you like to support me?'

Of course we all agreed. John Jenkins said that he was sure he saw a sparrow-hawk near his bird table recently. George Annett mentioned the sighting of a green wood-pecker, and my own decidedly inferior contribution was a pair of robins in my garden.

It was pelting with rain when we were about to depart. Henry offered John and me a lift to our respective doors, and we splashed away after sincere thanks for a splendid evening.

After we had dropped John we drove the quarter of a mile to my home. On the way Henry asked me what I thought of John.

'Very good-looking,' I replied. 'Good company too.'

'I think he's improved with age. Mellowed a bit. He was pretty insufferable at college.'

'Probably shy,' I replied, 'and throwing his weight about to prove that he wasn't. Lots of young people are like that.'

'Well, that's a charitable way of looking at it, I suppose.'

He was silent for a time, and then gave a gusty sigh as we drew up at my gate.

'Will you be seeing much of Jenkins?' he asked.

'I doubt it,' I replied, a little surprised. 'Until we all go to your meeting, I don't suppose our ways will cross.'

'Good,' said Henry, sounding much relieved, and drove off, leaving me to splash to my front door feeling mystified.

The next weekend was spent at Amy's and there, for the first time, I unburdened my recent troubles upon my old friend.

Amy took the whole affair rather more seriously than I did, and enquired about the tablets. Was I taking an iron tonic as she had suggested?

'Well, no,' I confessed, 'but the tablets may have iron in them.'

Amy looked sceptical, but did not pursue the issue.

'And you are taking care?'

'Yes, honestly. I was too frightened by the first business to do otherwise. I'm fine now.'

I proceeded to tell her, with some pride, of all my post-stroke activities, but she was not congratulatory, rather the reverse.

'You'll have another if you rush at things like a bull at a gate. You never learn, you know.'

She sighed, and looked sadly at me. 'I don't know what I'd do if anything happened to you. You mean a great deal in my life, and I don't like to see you in this sort of situation. Can't you retire?'

'Not while I'm fit. In any case, I gather from retired people that they work harder than ever when they have attained that happy state.'

'Rubbish!' retorted Amy. 'That's their own fault for

taking on far too many activities for comfort. I know how persuasive people can be, telling you it's only a once-a-month short meeting of this or that charity, and then you find there are half a dozen sub-committees and you are the chump of a chairman. James is always getting caught that way – and he hasn't even properly retired yet.'

'I promise not to fall into that trap,' I said meekly.

'My mother had a very slight stroke, I remember,' said Amy meditatively. 'She woke one morning and couldn't speak clearly. Luckily, she took it all as a great joke and in two days' time she was normal again. But we were all rather scared, I remember.'

'What age was she?'

'About our age, I suppose. My father took enormous care of her always, and we had about four doctors in the house within twenty-four hours. They had to stand up to a barrage of questions from my father. I should think they were glad to get out alive from our house.'

'Wonderful for your mother, though, to have such a champion.'

'Of course. That's one of the reasons I worry about you so much. If only you would marry some nice man. Henry, for instance. He's devoted to you, and he's so well-mannered.'

'So was Dr Crippen, I believe.'

'How provoking you are! Have you seen poor Henry since he returned?'

'Briefly. He is still very upset over his wife's death.'

I told her about the Annetts' party, and her eyes brightened at the thought of yet another man, John Jenkins, who might fall victim to my middle-aged charms. I decided to change the subject, and asked her to keep two dates free, one for our nativity play, and the other for our annual Christmas party.

'Does that include James too? I know he'd like to see the new children. As well as the old, of course,' she added.

I assured her that James would be more than welcome, and the question of a possible husband for me was shelved.

But only, I suspected, for the time being.

Rehearsals for the nativity play seemed to take up an enormous amount of time. The vicar had presented me with a list of services to be held in the church until the end of term, but pressed us to use the chancel at any other time for our rehearsals.

Consequently we trudged, twice, and sometimes thrice, a week through the churchyard to continue our preparations.

Somehow it always seemed to be raining, but nevertheless I found the churchyard a pleasant place, despite the dripping yew trees and the few rain-spangled upright cypress trees, so reminiscent of sunnier climes.

The grey tombstones glistened in the rain, and the magnificent square gravestone above the long-dead Sir Charles Dagbury, which listed to the north-east, dripped steadily from one side upon the wet clay runnel cut around it.

I thought of the seventeenth-century poet's line:

> *The grave's a fine and private place,*

and although I knew that Andrew Marvell was addressing 'His Coy Mistress', and that the next line was

> *But none I think do there embrace,*

nevertheless I relished the fineness and the privacy which I trusted that earlier Fairacre folk were now enjoying around me.

The church too had its usual calming effect on us all. It seemed pointless to worry about my health, fresh forms from the office, that ominous drip in the kitchen discovered that morning, Tibby's coughing attack and the present shortcomings of our rehearsals, when one considered that these ancient walls had witnessed the hopes and troubles of generations of Fairacre people. I think we all returned to school much refreshed in body and spirit after our efforts.

As always, the parents rallied splendidly to help us with costumes and props for the play.

The new Cotton girl was chosen to play Mary, and very good she was too, having natural grace, a sweet face and a clear voice. Mrs Cotton, her foster mother, sent over a blue frock which she hoped, in the little note attached, would be suitable for Mary's robes.

Unfortunately, it was heavily besprinkled with a flower pattern, and I was obliged to take it back after school.

To my surprise, she seemed unusually agitated about this.

'It's all I have,' she told me. 'Do you want me to buy some plain blue material?'

I assured her that it would not be necessary, as I thought that I might have a plain blue curtain at home which had once hung in Dolly Clare's bedroom, and would be ideal for draping round Mary.

She seemed mightily relieved, answered my inquiries about the children in a rather distracted way, and we parted amicably. As I returned, I told myself that she was probably anxious about a saucepan on the stove, or the toddler left sitting on an unseen chamber pot, and dismissed the matter from my mind.

The property box furnished us with a considerable amount of the costumes required. Mr Roberts, the local farmer and a school governor, provided hay for the box which represented the manger. The ox and the ass had been cut out of heavy cardboard years before, and had weathered their sojourn stuffed behind the map cupboard with remarkable endurance. Once dusted, and an eye redrawn, they were as good as new, we told each other.

The shepherds were clothed in dressing gowns, but here again it was quite a job to find suitably subfusc attire. Gaily patterned bath robes were paraded before us, sporting dragons, Disney characters and a panda or two. Where, I wondered, were the old-fashioned boys' camel-coloured numbers which I remembered from my youth?

After much searching we found one or two, and reckoned that the wardrobe and properties were at last complete.

We gave our first performance one afternoon in the last week of term. I was very grateful to the vicar for letting us have the beautiful chancel for our stage. Usually, any end of term function takes place in Fairacre school, and we are obliged to force back the wooden and glass partition between the two classrooms to make one large hall. Then there is the usual scurrying about for chairs from the school house and public-spirited nearby neighbours, not to mention some rickety benches from the village hall and the cricket pavilion which arrive on a trailer of Mr Roberts', and have to be manhandled into place for the great event, and manhandled back again to their usual home.

On this occasion our audience sat in the ancient pews and had a clear view of the chancel. Mr Bennett, the fosterfather at the first Trust's home, had emerged as an electrical wizard, and had volunteered to arrange temporary lighting. This threw the stage into sharp contrast with the dimness of the surrounding building, and gave the performance a wonderfully dramatic setting.

The play went without many hitches. At one point, the

cardboard ox fell down in a sudden draught from the
vestry door, and Joseph's crêpe beard came adrift from one
ear. This, however, was replaced swiftly by one of the
shepherds, hissing 'stand still, stand still!' whilst adjusting
the wire over his classmate's left ear, and we all waited for
the performance to continue.

It would not have been right to have a school affair like

this without some minor mishap, and we all thoroughly enjoyed ourselves.

The vicar closed the proceedings with a suitable prayer, and we filed out into the misty afternoon feeling all the better for celebrating, in our homespun way, the birth of Jesus.

The last afternoon of term was given over to our own school tea party. It has been the tradition at Fairacre for the pupils to entertain parents and friends. Amy and James were present.

Mrs Willet, who has the largest square baking tin in the locality, always makes the Christmas cake, and it is a job to get her to take the money for the ingredients. But this we insist on doing from the school fund, although I have never been allowed to pay her for the many eggs which go into it.

'I wouldn't *dream* of it,' she always says. 'They are our own hens' eggs, and it's our contribution to the party.' And so I am obliged to submit.

The cake usually has two robins, a church about the same size as the robins, and four Christmas trees, one at each corner, all standing in the snowy icing. Birds, church and Christmas trees are old friends and warmly welcomed each year, but on this occasion we had six attractive choirboys, about three inches high, all holding hymn books and obviously making the rafters ring from their open mouths.

'My neighbour brought them back from Austria,' said Mrs Willet proudly. 'I thought they'd make a nice change.'

Everyone agreed, although I think some of us rather agreed with Joseph Coggs who was heard to remark, 'Them robins was nicer!'

*

On Christmas Eve I drove to Bent to spend the Christmas holiday with Amy and James.

They were as welcoming as ever. The house was looking very festive with holly and ivy, and plenty of scarlet satin ribbon everywhere.

The three of us spent the first evening on our own, all of us glad of a few quiet hours after our Christmas preparations and before the busy day ahead.

Amy enquired anxiously about my welfare and I told her that I was now as fit as a fiddle, as right as a trivet, at the top of my form, and all the other descriptions of perfect health. She did not appear to be satisfied.

'Honestly, Amy,' I said, 'there's no need to worry about me.'

'Well, I do. I don't like the idea of your living alone. Anything might happen. By the way, I met your nice John Jenkins last week.'

'He's not *mine*,' I pointed out tartly, 'and I don't know him well enough to say that he is *nice*, but how did you come across him?'

'At a Caxley Society meeting. He gave a talk about an Elizabethan house he knew well, somewhere in Somerset. I was most impressed, and if it hadn't been such short notice I would have invited him to supper on Boxing Day.'

I knew that Amy had arranged this festivity for a few old friends, but was relieved to hear that John Jenkins was not to be present. Amy's match-making efforts are well meant, but decidedly obvious.

'What did you think of our nativity play?' I enquired.

Amy was enthusiastic, and I congratulated myself on steering her mind to another subject.

'And now tell me how you think the new families are settling,' said James, and I was able to give him an encouraging report on school progress.

We went early to bed, and I was asleep before half-past ten.

Christmas Day passed in the usual familiar pattern of present-opening, church service, turkey, plum pudding, siesta and a therapeutic walk after it.

We listened to the Queen, we agreed that a cup of tea was all that could be faced at four thirty, and Amy and I did a little desultory preparation ready for the next day's buffet supper.

I must say that twenty-four hours later, it looked remarkably elegant, spread out on a long table with a poinsettia in the middle of the starched white cloth.

Horace and Eve Umbleditch were there from Fairacre and two couples from near by in the village of Bent. We all moved about, plates in hand, catching up with the local news.

'Mrs Pringle called the other evening,' Eve told me. 'She was collecting prizes for the Fur and Feather Christmas whist drive, and practically asked me to show her over the school house.'

'And did you?'

'I didn't have much option. She approved of most of our alterations, and said that it was a lot *cleaner* than when you lived there. Horace said that I was not to tell you, but I knew you would relish a typically Pringle remark like that.'

I said she was right.

'What an old faggot she is,' went on Eve. 'She wanted to know how much the alterations had cost, and various other more personal matters such as had I been able to breastfeed my baby at my advanced age. Really, she takes one's breath away! On parting, she said she could always "help me out" if I wanted a cleaner.'

'I hope you put a stop to that offer.'

'I did!'

At that juncture Amy came round with some crackers for us to pull. The contents were unusually splendid, including pretty little brooches and key-rings and other baubles, but the reading of the enclosed riddles made the most fun.

They were all of the 'When is a door not a door? When it's a jar,' sort of standard, taking one back to one's comic-reading days.

Horace read his out to the assembled company, sounding mystified. 'Why is milk so quick?'

'"Why is milk so quick?"' echoed James. 'That doesn't make sense.'

'Neither does the answer,' said Horace, still bemused.

No one could offer any answer to the question and we all begged to be put out of our misery.

Horace read slowly, '"Because it's pasteurised before you see it."'

There were some groans and some laughter. Horace still looked perplexed.

'Pasteurised,' explained James. 'Past your eyes before you see it.'

'Good grief!' said Horace. 'Who thinks up these things?'

'Have another drink,' advised James. 'It'll take the taste away.'

I returned home after the break feeling relaxed and happy.

Tibby deigned to acknowledge me, which was unusual. Normally I have to make overtures with sardines or other acceptable peace offerings after an absence from home.

The weather was mild, and I wandered about the garden on that Wednesday morning admiring the beauty of bare winter branches silhouetted against a pale blue sky. A blackbird was busy scrabbling for grubs in the border, and somewhere in the distance, high above the downs, a lark was scattering its sweet notes. It was good to be back.

I went into the kitchen and put on the kettle to make coffee. Before I could put in the plug, a sharp pain shot through my head, and another through my chest.

The kitchen shelves, the table, the sink, all began to follow each other round and round in growing darkness.

It was almost a relief to hit the floor and give up.

PART TWO

SPRING TERM

CHAPTER 6

Should I Go?

It would be Mrs Pringle, of course, who found me.

She had gone to the school with a freshly washed pile of tea-towels ready for the start of term, and had found that the skylight was leaking, yet again, in my classroom.

She was hastening to catch the Caxley bus, before returning to Beech Green for her usual Wednesday 'bottoming' of my home. But she decided to drop off on the way to give me the news, and then to beg a lift from one of her Beech Green cronies who, she knew, always drove to Caxley about twelve on a Wednesday.

I must have lain there for about half an hour. She managed to support me to the couch in the sitting-room, and then rang the doctor.

It really was most providential that she had called in, at this unusual time, and although I dreaded the dramatic account which would soon be circulating around Fairacre and Beech Green, I was truly grateful for my old adversary's timely help.

I had tried to thank her but was frightened to find that my speech was most peculiar, and my tongue felt twice as large as usual. Also, the dreaded shaking had returned, and I was glad of the cup of tea Mrs Pringle held to my lips, and the rug she spread over me.

'I shall stop with you for the rest of the day,' she told me, 'and see the doctor in.'

She rose from the end of the sofa, and surveyed me sternly.

'May as well get on with the brights while we're waiting,' she said. 'I've never seen them candlesticks look so rough.'

She departed to the kitchen bearing them, and I heard drawers and cupboards being ransacked.

I lay there, bemused and shaken, to the accompaniment of Mrs Pringle's lugubrious contralto singing:

'Oft in danger, oft in woe.'

Very appropriate, I thought, wondering what the future held for me.

I must have dropped off for when I awoke I heard Mrs Pringle talking to someone in the kitchen.

'I thought to myself, "Well, Maud, if you nip into Caxley on the eleven, you can get the slippers at Freeman, Hardy & Willis and the brawn at Potter's for Fred's tea and catch the two o'clock back to Miss Read's for the brights.

'But that skylight was a blessing in disguise this time. "Best report that, I thought, and no time like the present," so I got off here and lucky I did.'

'It was indeed.'

I recognised Isobel Annett's voice.

'And there she was laying,' went on Mrs Pringle, (eggs or bricks, I wondered?) 'and my heart turned over. I thought she'd passed over, I really did.'

'I must see her,' said Isobel. 'Is she upstairs?'

'On the couch,' replied Mrs Pringle, sounding somewhat offended at being interrupted in her dramatic monologue.

Isobel came in, followed by Mrs Pringle. I had closed my eyes hastily. I could hear Mrs Pringle's breathing.

'I think we should get her to bed,' said Isobel.

I opened my eyes, and nodded, not daring to speak.

'Can you manage it?' asked Isobel, putting an arm round me. I nodded again, and we tottered entwined to the stairs, followed by Mrs Pringle.

'Could you make a little bowl of bread and milk?' asked Isobel. 'I think she might manage that.'

Mrs Pringle, debarred from the pleasure of undressing me, retired to do her allotted task.

She was limping heavily, I noticed, but was too concerned with my own troubles to worry much about it.

Dr Ferguson arrived and was reassuring.

'Luckily you haven't broken anything in the fall. And this is just another warning, like the first. It's simply hit other senses this time. I think your speech will be much better by the morning. The worst thing is this bang on the head, but it's coming up nicely.'

He fingered a lump on the right-hand side, making me wince.

'Stay there,' he told me, 'and I'll pop in tomorrow morning after surgery.'

I heard his car drive away. Some time, I thought dazedly, I should have to make all sorts of decisions. But not now. I was too tired to bother.

I turned my aching head upon the pillow, and fell asleep.

Amy came to look after me for a day or two, and then bore me back to her house at Bent with Dr Ferguson's blessing.

Normal speech returned within three or four days, and apart from the lump on my skull which diminished daily, and the overpowering feeling of exhaustion, I felt much as usual.

I wrote to thank Mrs Pringle, and also spoke to the vicar, telling him that I hoped to be fit to return to school as soon as term began. According to the doctor I had suffered from mild concussion, after my headlong collision with the cooker, as well as the second stroke which had triggered off the chain of events.

It was fortunate that all this had occurred in the holidays, but I had plenty of time, as I pottered about at Amy's, to consider the future. I had been given two 'warnings', as the doctor called them, in as many months. I had been lucky to get away with only a bump on the head as a secondary injury. As Dr Ferguson had said, I could have broken a leg or hip as I fell.

Memories of Dolly Clare's classroom collapse so long ago, and visions of other victims of strokes, all came to haunt me. My old dread of such an attack happening at school, in front of the children, was my chief anxiety, and I admitted this to Amy one quiet evening as we sat knitting by her fire.

I had marvelled at the way she had refrained from scolding me throughout her invaluable nursing, but now, confronting my fears, she spoke in her usual decisive manner.

'It's time you packed it in,' she said. 'I know you've only about two years to do, but whatever's the point in knocking yourself up, and starting retirement as an invalid?'

I said that the doctor had assured me that I should recover.

'He said that the first time,' retorted Amy, 'and you say yourself that you felt quite well, and did all the things he had told you, but even so you've had this second attack. To my mind, it's a more severe one. And with your speech affected what good would you be as a teacher?'

The same dismal thought had occurred to me, of course.

'Would you be terribly unhappy if you gave up your job?'

'I'd miss the children. But no, on the whole I think I'd enjoy being a free woman.'

'Have you got enough to live on? Would you have to wait to get your pension?'

'I've got quite a bit stashed here and there, and I'd have to find out more about the pension. I think I might get it immediately, but in any case, I can get by.'

'Well, James said that I was to tell you that we can tide you over, and you are not to worry.'

'James,' I said, 'is an angel in disguise.'

'Pretty heavy disguise too,' said Amy drily, 'when his breakfast's late.'

We shelved the problem of my future, and had a glass of Tio Pepé apiece.

A few days before term began I returned home. I felt

strong enough to face the rigours of school and my own
simple house-keeping. Tibby was somewhat stand-offish,
as might be expected, but came round after an extra large
peace offering of Pussi-luv.

My first visit was to Mrs Pringle to present her with a
china cake dish she had admired in Caxley, and had described to me some weeks before.

A rare smile lit up that dour face when she undid it, and
I renewed my thanks for her timely help.

'I truly thought you'd gone,' she told me. 'Like a corpse
you lay there, and I was going to straighten your limbs
before they stiffened, when you gave a groan.'

'That was lucky,' I commented.

'It certainly was! That's when I heaved you on to the
couch.'

'You were more than kind. And now I must be off.'

It was plain to me, as I met one or two old Fairacre
friends in the village, that my stroke had been well docu-
mented.

Mr Lamb at the Post Office shook my hand, and said it
was good to see me back. He did not actually add 'from
the dead', but I sensed it.

Jane Winter, one of the newcomers, said, 'My goodness,
I didn't expect to see you looking so well!'

Joseph Coggs, playing marbles outside the chapel, said
he thought I was still in hospital because I'd been struck
dumb. Mrs Pringle had said so to his auntie.

I replied in clear and rather sharp tones.

Mr Willet emerged from his gate, and entreated me to
come in, to sit down, to give him my coat, and to have a
cup of coffee which Alice was just making.

I accepted gratefully.

'Well,' said Bob, as we sat at the kitchen table with our

steaming mugs, 'I didn't believe half what Maud Pringle said, but we was all real scared to hear the news.'

'Not as scared as I was,' I told him. 'I'm not used to being ill.'

'You take care of yourself,' said Mrs Willet. 'We don't want anyone else in your place at the school. Everyone was saying so, weren't they, Bob?'

'So what's the news?' I asked hastily, changing the subject.

'Not much. Except for Arthur Coggs.'

'I thought he was safely in prison.'

'He come out about a fortnight ago. You know how it is these days. These villains get sent down for six months, and they're out again before you can draw breath. Remission, or some such. Anyway, he's out, and got one of his religious turns again.'

'Oh dear!' I exclaimed. We all know what havoc Arthur Coggs' religious turns can cause. On one occasion he had knocked up the Willets when they were asleep, and filled with burning zeal and too much strong beer had attempted to save their souls.

On another occasion he had entered the church during Evensong and started a loud tirade, punctuated with inebriated hiccups, on the after-life of those present in the congregation. Two sidesmen had removed him to the churchyard, but not before he had overturned a pot of gladioli in the church porch, and ripped a warning about swine fever from the noticeboard hard by.

On the present occasion evidently he had trespassed into the Women's Institute meeting at the village hall, whilst the members were engrossed in a cookery demonstration.

The demonstrator was a young woman with little experience. She was nervous before the twenty or so elderly women, who sat clutching their handbags on their laps and watching the proceedings with critical eyes. Her employers, a firm of flour manufacturers, had given her a course in pastry-making of all types, and this knowledge she was now imparting to her audience.

She had spent some time showing them different sorts of flour in half a dozen small bowls, and then continued with the making of choux pastry, puff pastry, and hot-water pastry for raised pork pies and the like. Whether she imagined that the women before her still ground their own flour from their harvest gleanings, no one could guess, but the rather condescending nature of her patter definitely irked them.

Had she but known, nine out of ten of those present had long ago given up making their own pastry, and rummaged in the local shops' refrigerator cabinets for nice ready-made packets marked 'shortcrust' or 'puff', and with no sticky fingers or mixing bowls to worry about.

It was while the earnest young woman was attempting to raise hot-water pastry round a jam jar that the interruption occurred.

It was not entirely unwelcome. The tea ladies were already beginning to whisper to each other about switching on the urn, when the door from the kitchen burst open, and Arthur Coggs, clearly the worse for drink, stumbled into the hall.

He approached the table unsteadily. The demonstrator, with a squeak of panic, retreated behind it, floury hands to her face in alarm.

'Get out, Arthur Coggs!' shouted one brave woman, but was ignored.

'Ish thish,' demanded Arthur, 'the 'all of shalvation?'

'No, it isn't,' said Mrs Partridge, the vicar's wife, coming forward to take charge as president. 'This is the village hall, and well you know it. Go home now!'

Arthur turned a bleary eye upon her. He put one hand on the table to steady himself, and smacked it down upon a wet mound of pastry.

'I've seen the light,' he began, amidst outraged murmurs. 'I bin a shinner, but now I'm shaved. And I'm going to shave you lot too.'

'Oh, no you're not, Arthur,' said Mrs Partridge firmly. 'You are going home, or we shall send for the police.'

She attempted to edge him towards the door. A large dollop of pastry fell to the floor, and was flattened under Arthur's boot.

'My pastry!' wailed the demonstrator, bending down to rescue it. The table gave a lurch from the activities around it, and the jam jar with its skirt of raised pastry rolled to join the mess on the floor.

'The police?' echoed Arthur. 'They needs to shee the light too.'

At this point, three more women came to Mrs Partridge's aid and manhandled the protesting saviour-of-souls into the kitchen.

'I'll just switch on while we're here,' said one, eminently practical, despite holding one of Arthur's ears.

Protesting vociferously, Arthur was bundled through the back door.

'I gotta meshage for you,' he shouted, 'a meshage from the Lord!'

'Well, you'd better go and tell the vicar,' replied Mrs Partridge, giving him a final push.

They slammed the door and bolted it.

'The idea!' puffed one.

'He ought to be put away!' said another.

'Won't the vicar mind?' queried the third timidly, as they went back to the hall.

'He can cope with Arthur,' replied Mrs Partridge. 'I have the WI on my hands.'

She swept in like a triumphant general at the head of his troops, and was greeted with cheers.

The New Year opened with a bitter wind blowing from the east.

The ground was iron-hard and white with frost until mid-morning. The ice on puddles scarcely had time to unfreeze during the day, before darkness fell at tea time and the temperature plummeted again.

Tibby and I went out as little as possible. Indoors we

were snug enough, for the fire burned brightly in this weather, and my new curtains kept out any draughts after nightfall.

I had plenty to do indoors. There were always school matters to deal with, as well as domestic jobs over and above the usual daily round. I turned out a store cupboard, marvelling at the low prices I had paid only a few years earlier, and even came across a tin of arrowroot which bore a label for one and ninepence. After such a length of time, the contents were given to the hungry birds. They appeared to be delighted with this vintage bounty.

As the first day of the spring term grew closer, I gave more and more thought to the future. Amy's advice about retirement was sensible, I realized, but it seemed so terribly *final*, the end of my useful life, so to speak, and with what would I fill my days?

On the other hand, was it fair to the school to struggle on with this constant dread at the back of my mind? I should not be the woman I was before these attacks, and I was reminded again, most uncomfortably, of the abilities of the new children in comparison with the indigenous Fairacre pupils whose accomplishments were not so high. Was it my fault? Were my teaching skills waning as I grew older? Was I pulling my weight?

There was no one that I could turn to to answer these questions. It was up to me to make a decision.

> '*There is a tide in the affairs of men,*
> *Which, taken at the flood, leads on to fortune,*'

I said to Tibby.

Tibby yawned again.

'Or, of course, *misfortune*,' I added. 'I might be a perfect fool to give up, and live till ninety in dire penury.'

Tibby yawned again.

'Which means,' I said severely, 'that you would have to live on *scraps*, and not Pussi-luv. And you would not be having the top of the milk, because we should both be on the cheapest sort, and in any case I should be *watering it down*!'

Oblivious to my warnings, Tibby rolled over to get the maximum benefit of the roaring fire, leaving me to wrestle with my doubts and fears.

The first day of term seemed even more bitterly cold than usual. I told myself that I had risen earlier and so the world was still in its night-time icy state.

The road to Fairacre was glassy, and the car did a few minor skids which could have been a problem if there had been traffic about. I drove slowly and was glad to enter the school playground and park the car.

Mr Willet had sanded the surface of the playground, for which I was grateful. I guessed that my pupils would not share my feelings, for there is nothing the boys enjoy more than a good long slide across the frozen asphalt, with a long line of them hurtling, one after the other, 'keeping the pot boiling'.

The school was warm. Mrs Pringle, resigned to the fact that winter was really here, had stoked up the two tortoise stoves and it was a joy to get indoors out of the bitter cold.

Mrs Pringle was flicking along the windowsill with a yellow duster, as I entered. She surveyed me morosely.

'You seem to have picked up,' she said. I thought she sounded a little disappointed.

'Thanks to you and other good friends,' I told her as cheerfully as I could.

'You want to keep in the warm,' she advised. 'The stoves is fair red hot.'

This was an over-statement, but I took it as a kindly gesture to a convalescent, as Mrs Pringle departed to the lobby.

It was good to be back. I looked round the empty classroom, with the bare shelves and nature table awaiting the fruits of the children's labours. The trappings of Christmas had gone. The paper chains, the Christmas tree, the nativity play, the school party, and all the other excitements of the end of term, were now behind us.

Here, in this empty and quiet room, I awaited the new term. Outside I could hear children's voices, and soon the room would be loud with the noise of children clamouring to tell me their news, scuttling from desk to desk, laughing, teasing and all sniffing from the cold world they had just left outside.

I went to let them in.

I had come to a compromise agreement with myself.

I would see how I coped with the first few weeks of term, and then decide whether I was fit to carry on or whether the sensible thing would be to retire.

A newly retired friend had mentioned that she had given in her notice before mid-February when she proposed to retire at the end of the school year in July. It seemed a long time to me, but when one considered that the post had to be advertised, applicants interviewed and *their* notices to be given in, it was absolutely essential to have this time in hand.

In a way, it helped me. I should have to make up my mind and stand by my decision. During that first week or two of term, I took stock. I felt well enough, but tired easily. I certainly did not have the burst of energy which followed my recovery from the first 'warning', but I was capable of teaching, doing my paperwork in the evenings,

and coping with everyday living. What I had to admit was
that I had really no resources of strength for any extra
crisis that might crop up.

I recalled several emergencies which had occurred at school
over the years. A child broke its leg, and I had to track down
the mother, take them both to hospital, and leave the school
for a good half a day to my assistant to run in my absence.

I myself had been smitten one day with a violent bilious
attack which involved many a hasty trip to the lavatory,
and eventually complete absence from school when I spent
the rest of the day in the school-house bathroom.

Then there were always minor crises in a building as old
as Fairacre school. The skylight alone was a source of
sudden upheavals involving instant attention. And beside
these structural defects there was the constant problem of
Mrs Pringle.

Matters came to a head one day towards the end of
January. The weather was still wickedly cold, but no snow
had fallen. Mrs Pringle moaned daily about the work it
made for her, the extra fuel needed for the stoves, the
journey along slippery roads to take up her duties, her bad
leg, the doctor's warnings, and so on.

Just before school dinner time one of the infants fell and
hit his head on the corner of a desk, and Mrs Richards and
I were hard put to it to stop the bleeding. We put as much
pressure as we safely could on the wound, while the poor
child screamed blue murder.

'You'd better take him into Caxley casualty,' I said, 'and
I'll track down his mother. I think she works at Boots.
She'll meet you at the hospital I expect.'

The two set off in Mrs Richards' car, the screams
slightly muffled by a boiled sweet from the school sweet
tin. I coped with my extended family of pupils, until my
assistant returned at two o'clock.

'They stitched him up, and he and his mother came home with me. He's much calmer, and has been put to bed. Look, it's begun!'

She pointed to the window, and there were whirling snowflakes, so thick that it was impossible to see the school house, my old home, across the playground.

We closed school early, and I had a nightmare journey over the few miles to Beech Green, for the roads seemed even slipperier than before, and the windscreen wipers could not cope adequately with the raging blizzard.

It was a relief to get indoors and to put the kettle on. As I drank my tea, I found that the old familiar shakes were back. Worse still, I was horrified to find that tears were coursing down my cheeks.

I replaced my cup with a clatter into the saucer, and leant back, defeated, in the chair.

This was it. It was time to go.

CHAPTER 7

The Die is Cast

Once I had made my decision I felt better immediately.

It was a Friday when school matters had come to a head and reduced me to such a demoralized condition. I spent the weekend contemplating the results of my overnight plans, and on the whole I felt mightily relieved.

Now and again, as I went about my weekend chores, I had twinges of doubt. Was it pride that made me loath to join my retired friends? Did I think that I was still as energetic and as capable as when I was appointed to be head teacher at Fairacre school? Did I imagine, when I surveyed myself in the looking-glass, that I looked younger and livelier than my contemporaries? Was I really able to cope with another two, or possibly more, years before I retired?

The honest answer to these questions was 'No'. Since my first stroke – mild or otherwise – I was not the robust and carefree woman that I had been. The second attack had robbed me of the small amount of self-confidence I had nurtured since the first. It was time to face reality.

And so I pottered about that weekend, and faced the future. February would begin in a day or two's time, and I should let the vicar know first, as head of the school governors and a dear friend of many years, just what I had decided to do.

Then I should confide in Mrs Richards, asking her to keep the matter to herself for a day or two while I composed a letter of resignation to the local authority.

I spent some time reviewing my financial arrangements. My newly retired colleague in Caxley had told me that my small teacher's pension would be paid as soon as I retired in July. I should also receive a substantial amount as my 'lump sum'.

This was comforting news. Moreover as I had told Amy, I had some savings in Caxley Building Society, and a wad of Savings Certificates somewhere upstairs, not to mention my useful Post Office book which was frequently raided in emergencies, but I had the inestimable good fortune of owning my own home, thanks to dear Dolly Clare's generosity. Few people, facing retirement, could be so happily placed.

I had no family problems, no husband or children to consider. I was my own mistress, and apart from the recent minor health setbacks, I was hale and hearty.

By the end of that weekend which had started so disastrously, I was beginning to look forward to my more leisured existence. Forewarned by my contemporaries, I should not make the mistake of being bounced into various village activities except those of my own choosing. But I should be able to be useful to my friends in various ways, babysitting for Eve and Horace Umbleditch, for instance, or running non-driving neighbours to Caxley when needed.

My ties with Fairacre would not be severed, for Bob Willet and Joseph Coggs would come to help in the garden, and Mrs Pringle would be with me every Wednesday until death did us part, I felt sure.

I went to bed on Sunday night facing a rosy future.

*

I had rung the vicar and asked if I might call after school on Monday.

'Come to tea,' had been the reply, and here I was pulling up outside the vicarage door which stood open hospitably.

'Tea first, and business later,' decreed Mrs Partridge, proffering buttered toast.

The fire crackled. Outside the birds were squabbling at the bird-table, an easterly wind ruffling their feathers and rattling the leaves of the laurels near by. It was good to be in the warm with old friends.

'Now tell us the news,' said Gerald Partridge when he had removed the tray to a side table.

I told them.

Dismay contorted their faces as I explained my plans, and I began to feel horribly guilty. But I soldiered on until the end of my monologue, and then waited for comment.

To my surprise, the vicar rose from his chair, enveloped me in an embrace and kissed me on both cheeks.

'What shall we do without you?' he cried.

'We shall have to manage,' said his wife resolutely, watching her husband return to his chair. She turned to me. 'It's a terrible blow, you know, but I'm sure you are doing the sensible thing. We've been so lucky to have you at the school for so long. And you've given us plenty of notice, thoughtful as always.'

'Won't you change your mind?' pleaded the vicar.

I shook my head. 'I've thought about it for ages,' I told him. 'I'm going to miss the school, but I feel I must go.'

'How we shall miss her,' he said, so mournfully that I felt he could not have been more cast down if I were emigrating to Australia.

'I shall only be at Beech Green,' I pointed out. 'And I hope you'll come and see me frequently with all my other Fairacre friends.'

They looked a little more cheerful, and we began to discuss the practical side of the matter.

'We have a governors' meeting this month,' said Gerald Partridge, 'so we can tell them then.'

I told him about sending in my resignation, and informing those involved. I think we were all feeling more settled when the time came for me to depart.

The wind was still whipping the bare trees, and sending flurries of dead leaves across the road, as I drove home. It was already dark, and it was plain that the night would be rough and cold. It was the weather to be expected in February, when the children had perforce to spend their playtime indoors and the lack of fresh air and exercise dampened the spirits of us all.

I looked ahead through the rain which now spattered the windscreen, at the windy road which led to home.

Before next winter, I told myself, I should be enjoying the comfort of my own fireside in the afternoons, while my successor coped with Fairacre school. And the skylight, of course. Not to mention Mrs Pringle!

I turned into my gateway in roaring high spirits.

It was during this bleak spell of weather that Henry Mawne gave his lecture on 'Birds of Prey' at Caxley.

Two days before the event John Jenkins rang up to say that he would give me a lift.

'Saves a lot of us wandering round trying to find a parking place,' he said. 'It begins at seven. Shall I pick you up at six thirty?'

'That's fine,' I said. 'Unless you'd like to come and have tea here first?'

'I should like that very much,' he said, and it was left that he would arrive at about five. I decided that it would be as well to provide something fairly substantial, such as crumpets, or sandwiches perhaps, so that we were fortified for Henry's evening.

The next day Henry rang.

'I'll pick you up at six,' he announced. 'Must get in a bit early to see about the plugs. Every hall I go to seems to have different electrical arrangements. Such a nuisance, but I have a first-class adaptor.'

I explained about John and invited him to join us.

'Well, that's cool, I must say,' spluttered Henry. 'He knows we made the arrangements last time we met. I said I'd pick you up.'

He sounded genuinely put out, and I tried to make amends.

'Honestly, Henry, I don't remember us making a set date. I'm sorry if it throws out your plans. Can't we all go in together?'

'No, we can't,' he snapped. 'Leave it as it is, now you've made this muddle with John. I'll see you after the meeting.'

He rang off, leaving me thoroughly cross. I was positive that we had made no arrangements to meet, and in any case, that was weeks before when we had met at the Annetts' party. How like a man to put the blame on me! And if he resented my inviting John Jenkins to an innocent cup of tea, he must just get on with it. I had plenty to occupy me without worrying about foolish old men who behaved like infants.

What a blessing it was to be a spinster!

In no time, of course, it was the talk of Fairacre that I was going to retire.

Mrs Richards' eyes filled with tears when I told her, and I was obliged to find the box of tissues kept for infant eyes and noses to put her to rights again.

'I think I'll give up myself,' she wailed. 'I honestly can't face working with anyone else.'

I did my best to brace her, and before long she was herself again, much to my relief. What would the children think if *all* the staff – both of us – resigned at the same time, I said?

Bob Willet said everyone would grizzle about me going but he and Alice had said for a long time I was looking peaky and I worked too hard. I rather enjoyed the last part of his remarks. I so rarely get the chance to feel a martyr.

Mrs Pringle responded typically. It was her opinion, she told me, that I should have gone months ago. (My enjoyment of Bob Willet's assessment of my worth vanished immediately.)

'You've been off-colour ever since that first funny turn,'

she continued. 'Shaking like a jelly. Tripping over things. Forgetting to shut the skylight. Sharp with the kiddies. Pecking at your good school dinner. I said to Fred, long before Christmas, "You mark my words, Fred, she'll either crack up and end in the county asylum, or the doctor'll make her see sense and retire." Those was my very words.'

'Well, luckily,' I said, as mildly as I could in the face of this tirade, 'I'm taking the second course. So far, at least.'

Mr Lamb at the Post Office said that I would be sorely missed, and maybe they would appoint a man next time which might make some of the children mind their Ps and Qs. This left me wondering how far my disciplinary powers had deteriorated in the past months and if, perhaps, I should have given in my notice years before.

But on the whole, I received nothing but kindness from my Fairacre friends and parents, and far more compliments than I deserved. Perhaps one had to go before one was really appreciated? I was reminded of the glowing obituary notices in *The Caxley Chronicle* dwelling on the sterling merits of local characters 'beloved by all'.

The children, of course, were much more realistic, wondering if my retirement would mean a half-holiday for them, who would take my place, and was I going because I was too old? Or was I *really* ill?

'You're not going to die?' queried Joseph Coggs interestedly.

'Not just yet,' I assured him.

John Jenkins proved to be good company. He had travelled in many countries, and had a cottage in the south of France which he visited for several months of the year.

His Beech Green house was providing him with plenty of household repairs, and these he seemed to be enjoying.

The Annetts had told him about my proposed retirement, and he asked me about my plans.

'I shall enjoy feeling free,' I told him. 'I look forward to visiting friends, and parts of the country I haven't yet seen.'

'Won't you miss the work? The routine? Setting off at the same time each day, and so on?'

'Good lord, no! Why, do you?'

'I did at first,' he admitted, 'but then I think men find it harder to adjust to retirement than women.'

I pondered this as I poured out our second cups of tea. There was truth in the statement. I could think of half a dozen men of my acquaintance, usually successful business men, who had been unsettled and irritable in the first months of retirement, nearly driving their wives mad.

'Women have wider interests, I suppose,' I answered. 'Everyday jobs like cooking and housework, and all the things that have to be looked after in a house. So often a man devotes himself to just one aim, like building up a business, or running an efficient office. When that's taken away he feels lost.'

'I certainly went through that stage. Felt useless, finished, chucked aside. That's why I took on so many voluntary jobs in the village. Too many, I realise now. Don't you make that mistake.'

I promised that I would not, and soon afterwards we set out to the school hall in Caxley where Henry was to give his lecture.

He came bustling up to meet us as we entered, and I was relieved to see that he appeared in excellent spirits.

'Everything in splendid form here,' he cried. 'The head-master was absolutely spot-on about the electrical equip-ment. And two sixth form boys to do the heaving about. By the way, I've booked a table for supper after the show. At the White Hart, if that suits you?'

We thanked him warmly and found our seats.

The hall filled up very satisfactorily, considering how bleak and unpleasant a night it was. Left alone I should have stayed by my fire. Obviously a great many people were more public-spirited.

The lecture on 'Birds of Prey' was vaguely familiar, and I recalled that Henry had given a simple version of it to our school some time before. We had followed it up by paying a visit to a Cotswold falconry, and a good time had been enjoyed by all.

Henry spoke well, and the slides were magnificent. There is something primitively splendid about the fierce eyes and cruel beaks of eagles, kestrels and the like which compel fear as well as admiration. We all sat enthralled, and although Henry's lecture lasted well over an hour no one fidgeted.

Half an hour later we were sitting at a table in Caxley's premier hotel, a comfortable old building, once a coaching stop, with ample stabling at the rear.

As well as Henry and John, the headmaster and his wife were present, and the master who had been instrumental in getting Henry to give the lecture.

'I hear you are retiring soon,' he said to me.

'At the end of the school year probably,' I replied, marvelling yet again about the dispersal of news.

'Well, if you want something to do,' he went on, 'I can find you a little job publicising the work of our local nature society. Very worthwhile, and you would meet lots of people.'

'I've often seen you at concerts,' broke in the headmaster, 'and I know you are fond of music. Do come and hear our school orchestra one day.'

'And you must join our Ladies' Club,' added his wife. 'We meet every third Wednesday of the month, and have really first-class speakers. Some of them charge over a hundred pounds, so you can see we get only the best.'

I began to see how tough I should have to be to resist all the pressure about to engulf me.

John Jenkins came to my rescue. 'I've already warned her about taking on too much when she retires,' he remarked.

'And so have I,' added Henry. 'There will be quite enough scope for her in Beech Green and Fairacre, I'm sure.'

'We'll return to the attack later,' said the headmaster, with a smile, and I was thankful that the conversation turned to rugby prospects for the rest of the season, and I could enjoy my excellent meal without harassment.

I was pleased to see Henry so jovial again, for although he had annoyed me by assuming such a possessive air when he had rung me about driving in, I was sorry to have upset him unwittingly. He was still in a sad state after losing his wife, and I did not want to hurt him further.

But my complacency was short-lived. At the end of the evening, after we had said goodbye to the Caxley contingent, Henry turned to me and said, 'Shall we set off then?'

'I can run her back,' said John quickly.

'No need. I pass the door,' responded Henry.

'Don't you worry,' replied John. 'You've got to unpack all your gear when you get back to Fairacre.'

I began to feel like a bone between two dogs. Both men were getting pink in the face.

'I'm afraid I left my gloves in John's car,' I faltered.

'In that case,' said John swiftly, 'you had better come back with me, as arranged.'

Henry took a deep breath, turning from pink to crimson in the process. 'Very well,' he managed to say, 'if it's *arranged* then there's nothing to say, is there?'

'Thank you for a really lovely evening,' I said weakly, but found that I was addressing his back.

John took my arm in an irritatingly proprietorial manner, and we made our way to the hotel car park. I was sorry that the evening had ended so unhappily, and said so to John as we emerged into the road.

'He'll get over it,' he said dismissively. 'The trouble with Henry is that he's such an old woman. Always was.'

I felt that this was as unkind as it was churlish. After all, Henry had arranged the evening, given us a first-class dinner, and been a genial host until the last few wretched minutes.

We continued our journey in silence. The headlamps lit up the hedges and grass verges glistening with a hard frost. An owl flew across our path intent on finding prey in this harsh world.

As we approached Beech Green, I roused myself enough to give John polite thanks for the lift, and he responded, equally politely, about tea.

'I will see you in,' he said as we drew up at my gate.

'Please don't bother,' I said. 'You have been most kind, and as you see, I have left the light on.'

We wished each other good night, and off he went, much to my relief.

For the time being anyway, I had had quite enough of John Jenkins' company.

In the week following our Caxley evening, more snow fell. Luckily, it was not too heavy, but the ground was so iron-cold and hard that it lay for several days without thawing much.

The children's Wellingtons stood in a row in the porch, but I was surprised to see that the oldest Cotton girl, who had played Mary so beautifully in our nativity play, was the only child in shoes. Naturally, they were soaking wet, and I put them near the stove to dry.

'What's happened to your Wellingtons?' I asked. The two younger boys had come to school in theirs.

'Too small, miss,' she replied. 'Mum's getting me some in Caxley on Saturday.'

'Her shoes are too small as well,' piped up one of her brothers, and the girl flushed with annoyance.

'Well, you all grow fast at this stage,' I said cheerfully, 'and run your poor parents into a lot of expense.'

An odd look passed between the two children. A warning? Fear? Embarrassment? There was no telling, but we continued with our work and I soon forgot about this transitory and uneasy feeling.

February began as cheerless as the last few days of January had been. Consequently my bird table was thronged with finches of all colours, as well as robins and sparrows. Beneath it the blackbirds and hedge sparrows bustled about, and on one occasion a spotted woodpecker joined the gathering, scaring the small birds away from the peanuts which he attacked energetically with his powerful bill.

But by mid-month a welcome change occurred. The wind veered to the south-west, the air became balmy, and the last vestiges of snow, which had lain beneath the hedges, gradually melted away.

Our spirits rose steadily with the temperature. For one thing, the children could go outside to play, which was a relief to us all. The evenings were drawing out. It was possible to have a walk, or for the children to play outside, after tea, and the curtains were drawn at around six o'clock rather than four.

My resignation had gone to the office, and I had received an extremely kind and flattering letter from the Director of Education, no less. I was beginning to wonder if I had done the right thing by resigning.

Just as one feels much better when one has rung the dentist for an appointment and the pain stops immediately, so I felt now. The relief at having made a decision – even if it were the wrong one – was overwhelming.

I did not have many of these twinges of doubt. I knew only too well that the course I was pursuing was the right one.

Amy was particularly helpful at this time. She called one afternoon when I had just returned from school, and we had tea together. The window was open, and the curtains stirred in the warm breeze. A bowl of paper-white narcissi scented the room. Spring had come at last.

'I get restless at this time of year,' said Amy, lighting a cigarette.

'It's time you gave up smoking,' I told her. 'Don't you read about all the horrors it does to your lungs, not to mention unborn babies?'

'I'm not too bothered about my lungs after all these years, and there never have been any babies to worry about, worse luck.'

I felt a pang of remorse. Amy and James would have made ideal parents, but Fate had deemed otherwise. It was one of the reasons, I guessed, that James was so exceptionally good in dealing with the children and their parents in the Trust housing scheme.

'Easter's early this year,' went on Amy, blowing a perfect smoke ring. 'What are you doing?'

'Getting the outside painting done. Wayne Richards says he'll come as soon as we break up.'

'Is that your assistant's husband? The one with the handsome beard?'

'The very same,' I told her.

'And how long will he need to paint the outside?'

'Lord knows. A week, I suppose. Why?'

'James is off on another Trust venture around Easter. I think he hopes to find a house or two in the Shropshire area – lovely part of the country. I wondered if you would like to keep me company.'

'It sounds lovely.'

'No need to make plans yet. I'll have to fit in with James's arrangements, but bear it in mind.'

I promised enthusiastically, and we went out to look at the garden.

It was a cheering sight after the past gloomy weeks. The green noses of innumerable bulbs had pushed through the wet earth. The lilac buds were as fat as green peas, and the honeysuckle was already in tiny leaf.

In one corner I had planted dwarf irises, *reticulatum* and *danfordiae*, and already the purple flowers of the former and the cheerful yellow ones of the latter were making a brave show now that the weather had changed.

Only the ancient trees remained bare, but even so I felt that there was a haziness in their all-over aspect, as if the buds were beginning to swell and ready to burst very soon into the glory of Spring.

Amy sniffed rapturously.

'Bliss, isn't it?' she said.

'It is indeed,' I replied.

CHAPTER 8

Medical Matters

The spring term is not my favourite of the school year. The weather is at its most malevolent, and children's complaints such as whooping cough and measles seem to crop up in the early months with depressing regularity.

This year was no exception, despite the natural robustness of the Fairacre young. The two Cotton boys succumbed to measles and two of the Bennett children next door were also casualties. Joseph Coggs was absent too with influenza, which would no doubt spread to the rest of the family.

Mrs Pringle, relishing the news of each new sufferer, added her own contribution to the list.

'Minnie's Basil has got the croup. Cough, cough, cough, and what he brings up you'd never believe.'

I attempted to escape from these horrors into the lobby, but was confronted by her bulk.

'And she's expecting again,' she added.

'What? Minnie?'

'Who else?'

'But the baby can't be more than a few months,' I protested.

'Twelve. No, I tell a lie. Must be fourteen months now.'

Frankly, I was appalled at the news. Minnie Pringle, Maud's scatterbrained niece, has the mentality of a twelve-year-old and is already the mother of several children, and stepmother to four or five of her husband's by his former marriage. How they all manage to eat and sleep, and even breathe comfortably in their Springbourne council house, has always been a mystery to me.

'Ern's turned nasty about it,' continued Mrs Pringle.

'He might have thought of that before,' I replied tartly.

'He don't reckon it's his,' said Mrs Pringle.

This took the wind out of my sails, of course. Come to think of it, reason told me, Ern might well be right. Minnie's relationships with the opposite sex were always remarkably haphazard.

'But he must know, surely,' I said. 'And Minnie must know.'

'She don't rightly remember,' said Mrs Pringle, taking a swipe with her duster at my desk and thereby removing the hymn list for the month.

I stooped to pick it up, trying to come to terms with Minnie and Ern's attitude to parenthood. The trouble with me is that I constantly try to rationalize matters. When one is dealing with the Minnies and Erns of this world reason does not come into it, but I never learn.

'So what's happening?'

'Well, Ern give her a good hiding for a start, but he's letting her stay, and says the baby'd better look like him, and not that Bert, or there'll be real trouble.'

At the mention of Bert, one of Minnie's more persistent admirers, my heart sank. I had once had to face him in my own schoolroom, and very unnerving the encounter was.

'But surely,' I protested, 'she isn't still seeing Bert? I thought he'd moved to Caxley and broken with her.'

'There's always the bus,' said Mrs Pringle. She began to move towards the door.

'Mind you,' she said, 'I don't hold with all our Minnie

does, but when it comes to *love* there's nothing to be done. Minnie's always had a loving nature, and Bert always came first. Ern don't seem to understand that.'

She disappeared, leaving me exhausted with other people's problems.

My own particular problem that day was a visit to the doctor's surgery for a routine check-up.

The waiting-room was full, as always, and I had my usual difficulty in choosing reading matter from the pile provided. Should it be a ten-year-old copy of *Autocar, The Woodworker*, or last Easter's copy of *Woman and Home*?

I settled down with this last offering and soon became absorbed in the cooking pages. Why didn't my steak and kidney pies turn out like the one in the picture? Mine always collapsed round the pie funnel, leaving a white china steeple arising from the ruined pastry roof around it.

Two women were busy discussing the reasons for their presence. One had a straightforward boil on her neck which was covered with a large sticking plaster.

I felt truly sorry for her, particularly as she was getting scant sympathy from her friend who had far more interesting symptoms to describe.

There are times when I curse the fact that my hearing is so good. Give the woman her due, she spoke in low tones as befitted the intimate nature of her disclosures, but I could hear every word.

'It's a blockage, you see, dear, in the *tubes*. They lead to the womb and all that part. In the privates. I never remember the name of the tubes.'

Mrs Pringle, I recalled, named them 'Salopian tubes', which had a nice healthy, if erroneous, air of Shropshire about them.

'So what will they do?' enquired the friend, now resigned

to the fact that her boil was of very little consequence in the face of such competition.

Her companion's voice dropped even lower. 'Dilation, I expect. And then blowing out.'

'I don't like being messed about with down there,' said her friend primly.

'Well, I can't say I *relish* it,' agreed the other, 'but needs must when the devil drives, as my old mamma used to say.'

She began to rummage in an enormous handbag.

'I cut out a bit from the woman's page of the *Mirror*. It was all about this business. I brought it along for the doctor to see. It might give him a lead, I thought. He's only young.'

I wished I could be an invisible witness at this confrontation, but at that moment my name was called, and I had to leave this gynaecological saga behind me.

Dr Ferguson was as welcoming as ever, but looked decidedly careworn. He was going to look a jolly sight more so, I thought, when the tubes-lady took my place.

'And how do you feel?'

'Splendid. No problems.'

'Good. I'll just take your blood pressure.'

He got out the paraphernalia from a drawer and began to wind the soft stuff round my arm. Why such a simple action should be so unpleasant I have no idea, but as the band tightens I am always convinced that I am about to be asphyxiated.

Reason tells me that I am being absurd. The contraption is nowhere near my throat and lungs. Nevertheless, panic rises in me, and I feel that I should tell the doctor to knock off the top five or six degrees of whatever the thing is registering, on account of my acute cowardice.

'Fine,' he said, releasing me from my bonds. 'Down quite a bit. Tablets are working well.'

There were a few routine questions. Tongue, eyes, neck glands were examined, and I was about to escape when he said, 'I hear you're retiring. Will you have plenty to do?'

'More than enough,' I assured him.

He sighed. 'You see, I always think that you single women *need* a job. To make up for the lack of motherhood, you understand. Women *need* motherhood.'

I thought of Minnie. She ought to be the picture of health and serenity at this rate.

'They need children to *fulfil* themselves biologically. It's not just "the patter of tiny feet", I don't mean that.'

'I get plenty of the patter of not-so-tiny feet,' I said. 'Thirty-odd children, from five to eleven years of age, make a pretty deafening patter on bare boards.'

'I'm sure of that.' He began to look less worried, to my relief. I did not want to add to his professional cares on my behalf.

'Honestly, I'm looking forward to retirement now. And if I find that I miss the children, I can always pop into school for a visit. Not that I shall do that very often. I'm planning to be too busy to look back.'

He smiled, and looked his usual cheerful self. I felt virtuously that I had done him good, as I made for the door.

The tubes-lady was rising from her chair, the *Mirror* cutting in hand.

Poor chap, I thought, as I departed. That will give him a relapse, after all my rallying efforts on his behalf.

As I lay in bed that night waiting for sleep, I pondered on my doctor's attitude to single women.

It was obvious that he felt that we were to be pitied. We

had missed one of the most wonderful experiences in life. We were, in that ghastly phrase, 'unfulfilled'.

What made him think in this way? Was it a dislike of *waste*? Here I was, for example, a perfectly healthy – well, nearly – specimen of normal womanhood, with all the right interior equipment, I imagined, for reproduction, the tubes, orifices and appropriate spaces, but they had not been called upon to function.

This did not worry me, so why should it worry him? When I thought about it, I felt I had got off lightly in the reproduction stakes. So many of my married friends told me, in nauseating detail, of their experiences of childbirth, that I was glad I was spared the experience.

I could truthfully say that I had never missed having children. When I watched my friends coping with the problems of babyhood, sleepless nights, changing nappies, enduring the screams of teething, and then the later traumas of childhood illnesses, and the still later, and still more anxious, perils of their children's teens, I felt that I was lucky indeed.

Of course, I realised that I had a full-time job with children which might unconsciously have compensated for my spinsterhood. I was glad that I had reminded my kind-hearted doctor of this.

But why, if it were not the waste of my organs which upset him, was he still unhappy?

Could it be that he was *romantic*? So many men are. We are brought up to believe that it is the female of the species that has the hearts-and-flowers attitude to love, who craves attention and decks herself to catch a mate. In fact, it is the other way round. It is the male who brings flowers and chocolates, and dresses himself in fine array.

Take pigeons, for instance, or any other bird. The female is happily pottering about pecking up her breakfast, and the male bird is in a state of wild excitement, his ruff bristling, head down as he circles, making amorous rumblings from the throat. The female takes no notice. She has quite enough to do at the moment, and her wooer's attentions are rather a nuisance. She is definitely not the romantic one.

My thoughts drifted to Minnie Pringle. What would happen to her and that large family? Ern had been warned some time earlier by the police when he had attacked one of his wife's admirers. Poor Minnie was a fool, but more sinned against than sinning, and I was sorry for the children of that stormy household.

Well, I thought, snuggling down into my comfortable bed, maybe it would all blow over and I should hear no more of Minnie's troubles.

But there I was wrong.

Bob Willet was putting a new washer on the tap when I arrived at school the next morning. He broke off to greet me.

'Never had this bother when I was at school here. Just had buckets of water.'

'There were buckets when I came,' I told him. 'And a fine old nuisance they were. Trying to keep the flies out was enough for me.'

'Arthur Coggs put a frog in one once,' he reminisced.

'He would.'

'Did you know there's a toad as lives up Mr Mawne's?'

'Have you seen it?'

'Dozens of times. Mr Mawne's put two pieces of slate lodged by his front door to make a little home for him. But he's not there now.'

'What, the toad? Is he hibernating?'

'No, no. Mr Mawne. He's in Ireland for a week or two,

seeing his relations. I'm doing the greenhouse while he's gone.'

'I hadn't heard.'

'You will,' said Bob, as he departed.

'Henry Mawne is away at the moment,' said the vicar when he came to take prayers. 'He asked me to keep it quiet, as it doesn't do to advertise the fact that the house is empty these days.'

'Isn't his housekeeper there?'

'No. She's having a break too.'

Mrs Pringle arrived later to wash up.

'So Mr Mawne's away in Ireland. I wouldn't want to have that crossing in this weather.'

Mr Lamb at the Post Office was more forthcoming still.

'Mr Mawne flew from Bristol. Don't take more than a few minutes to get to Cork. We'll miss him around for the next fortnight.'

Alice Willet, Jane Winter and Mrs Richards all wanted to know if I had heard that Mr Mawne had gone to Ireland.

So much for keeping things quiet in a village.

That same evening John Jenkins rang.

'Have you ever been to Rousham?' he enquired.

'Never. Where is it?'

'It's between Bicester and Chipping Norton. North of Oxford. A lovely place, and not far to go. I rang to see if you would care to go to a concert there.'

'How lovely! When?'

'It's rather short notice. Next Wednesday? I'd pick you up about six. The concert begins at seven thirty. It's in aid of the RSPB.'

'Oh! I suppose Henry might be there.'

'He's away in Ireland.'

'Of course. I had forgotten.'

We gossiped for a little about this and that, and he rang off.

Now what, I wondered, would one wear on a February night to a charity concert in an old house?

Something warm, I decided, and went to bed.

Mrs Pringle was just finishing her Wednesday chores when I got home that afternoon.

'I've done out under your stairs,' she announced, 'and not before time. There was a spider in there as big as a crab.'

'Good heavens!'

'And that ironing board of yours fell down again and hit my leg something cruel. You want to put that thing somewhere else.'

'But where? I have thought about it.'

'If it was my contraption I'd put it in the garage.'

Actually, I thought, that's not a bad idea.

'I'll put on the kettle,' I said, 'and I'll run you home a mite early. I'm out this evening.'

'Ah yes!' she said smugly. 'Out with Mr Jenkins, I hear. You'll have to see Mr Mawne don't get jealous.'

I pretended that I had not heard above the noise of the water running into the kettle, but my heart sank. I supposed it was all over the neighbourhood that I was pursuing a lone widower, if not two.

We drank our tea, and kept the subjects to such harmless topics as the ever-present influenza, the exorbitant price of seed potatoes, how much a Caxley decorator had asked for doing out the village hall, and so on.

John Jenkins was only mentioned again, as I drove her back to Fairacre.

'He's a nice-looking man,' said Mrs Pringle. 'He reminds me of the rent-collector as used to come regular to my auntie's in Caxley. Very civil he always was, and my auntie never failed to say what a pleasure it was to hand over the rent money every week.'

I made an appreciative noise.

'We was all surprised when he was took away for murdering his poor wife. Done it with a common meat cleaver too.'

Mrs Pringle sounded aggrieved, as though such a good-looking civil man could at least have picked a worthier weapon, such as a cavalry sword, for the job.

Driving back I hoped that John Jenkins, who looked so like the rent-collector, did not have the same murderous urgings.

Too late now to worry about it anyway, I decided, as I looked out suitable raiment for the outing.

It was a lovely evening. It was still light enough to see the countryside as we drove north, and the air was balmy.

John was an easy companion, and we had plenty to talk about. He obviously enjoyed music, played the flute, and was wondering if the Caxley orchestra would welcome him next season.

It was dusk when we arrived at Rousham, but the bulk of the house against the sunset glow looked interesting, and I said so.

'It is. We'll come again in the summer. It's the garden here that is the main attraction. It was laid out by William Kent early in the eighteenth century, and is pretty well unchanged. He had a lot to do with the house too. It's one of my favourite places. We'll make a definite date, as soon as it opens.'

The concert took place in the hall, and was just the sort

of music I like, a quartet playing melodious pieces of Schubert, Mozart and Haydn, a delight to the ear and enabling one to let the mind drift happily.

At the interval we ate delicious snippets of this and that with plenty of smoked salmon and prawns and luscious pâtés around, and red and white wine flowing copiously.

Some of us went outside and stood on the steps, for the night was pleasantly warm. The stars were out, and a light breeze rustled William Kent's ancient trees.

As we returned we met two Caxley friends, Gerard Baker and his wife Miriam. As Miss Quinn, she had lived for a time in Fairacre, and was a good friend of mine. Introductions were made, and Miriam and I caught up with local gossip, leaving the men behind.

'I hear you are retiring.'

I told her why. She was sympathetic and sensible.

'You won't regret it. As you know I go back occasionally to help out if Barney wants me, but as time passes, I really don't want to leave all my little domestic ploys.'

I said I could well understand that. I did not imagine that my life would suddenly become empty.

She laughed and agreed. 'It won't be, I assure you,' she said, as we made our way back to our chairs. '"Nature abhors a vacuum", as my old science teacher taught us.'

A tag to remember, I thought, as the music began again.

March, which is reputed to come in like a lion and go out like a lamb, was doing the thing in reverse.

Not that anyone complained. The gentle weather, which had been so much appreciated on the Rousham evening, continued to bless us, and the influenza and other patients returned in a straggle to their duties at Fairacre school.

I took them for a shorter nature walk than usual one afternoon, in deference to their debilitated condition. We

found catkins, of course, which had been fluttering in the hazel hedges for several weeks, but also some real harbingers of spring in the shape of coltsfoot, violets and one or two early primroses.

Joseph Coggs found a blackbird's nest, and we all had a quick peep, but hurried off as the male bird kept up an outraged squawking from a nearby holly tree, and we did not want his bright-eyed mate to desert the eggs.

'Soon be Easter,' said Ernest. 'My mum said Mr Mawne's going to have an egg hunt.'

This sounded odd to me. After all, Henry is a keen ornithologist, and an egg hunt sounded wrong. I must have looked puzzled.

'*Chocolate* eggs,' explained Ernest. 'All over the garden, and then a lantern show in the village hall.'

'That's very kind of Mr Mawne,' I said. This was the first I had heard that he was back in Fairacre. 'You will be going to both, I suppose?'

Ernest sighed. 'Well, my mum said you can't just collect the chocolate eggs and not go on to the lecture, so I suppose I'll have to go.'

Well done, mum, I thought!

As we passed the churchyard there was the sound of a spade at work. We looked over the wall to see Bob Willet digging at the bottom of a grave. He looked pink and cheerful.

'You lot playing truant again?' he asked, straightening up from his labours.

'Look! Two primroses!' shouted Patrick.

'And six violets!' called one of the Bennett boys.

'And we know where there's a blackbird sitting,' said Joseph.

'I can do better'n that,' replied Bob Willet. 'There was a grass snake sunning itself on my compost heap midday.'

'Can we go and see it?'

'He scarpered when he saw me. But it shows the spring's come. You'll have to look out for frogs' spawn before long.'

We waved him goodbye and returned with our treasures to the school.

This, I thought with a pang, would be the last time I should see the nature table decked with the bounty of spring. Where should I be when it came again?

I shook myself out of this melancholy mood.

Busy as ever, no doubt, for didn't Nature abhor a vacuum?

Amy rang me that evening to tell me about the plans for our Easter break in Shropshire.

'James has found a very nice country hotel, not far from Bridgnorth. The only snag is that we shall have to be there over the Easter weekend. It's the only time he can see the business man, evidently. He's abroad most of the time, but is nipping over to see his mother in Shrewsbury for the holiday weekend.'

'It's fine by me, Amy. I'm looking forward to it.'

'So am I. We'll pick you up on Good Friday morning then, and come back on Monday afternoon. Suit you?'

'Perfectly.'

'And did you enjoy the concert at Rousham?'

'How did you know about that?'

'I met Miriam and Gerard in Caxley. They said you were there.'

Was *anything* private, I wondered sourly?

'With that handsome John Jenkins,' continued Amy.

'That is quite correct,' I replied.

'Oh, good!' said Amy, with unnecessary enthusiasm. 'See you on Good Friday morning then, if not before.'

She rang off, and I went to close the kitchen window. The wind had sprung up, and squally rain showers were on the way, according to the radio weather man.

It was almost dark when I heard someone knocking at

the front door. Normally people come to my back door, usually calling out as they come.

I opened the door to find John Jenkins there, with a book in his hand.

'Come in out of this wind,' I said.

'I thought you might like to look at this. There's a nice account of Rousham in it.'

It was a handsome volume dealing with country houses and I said that I should enjoy reading it.

I rather hoped that he would depart. His car was at the gate, and I imagined that he was on his way elsewhere. However, he lingered, and I invited him to sit down, and offered coffee. The children's marking would have to wait.

While the kettle boiled I rummaged in a very superior square biscuit tin, a Christmas present, and wondered why the lids of square biscuit tins never go on properly first time. Almost as frustrating, I thought, pouring boiling water on to the coffee, as those child-proof medicine containers where you have to align two arrows in order to prise off the lid. So useful in the middle of a dark night. And anyway, a child could undo the thing with far more ease than I could.

John was well settled into an armchair, but leapt up politely as I entered.

He seemed very much at ease and admired the cottage. I told him how lucky I had been to inherit it.

'You must come and see mine,' he said. 'Are you busy next week?'

I told him that the end of term was looming up, and perhaps I might be invited during the Easter holidays?

He brought out a pocket diary immediately, and my heart sank at such efficiency. I could see that there would be no escape.

The Thursday or Friday after Easter was fixed for me to take tea at his house, and half an hour later he left.

By now, the rain was lashing down. In the light from the porch it slanted in silver rods across the wind-tossed shrubs.

He ran down the wet path, raised his hand in farewell, and a moment later the car moved off.

Thankfully, I removed the tray and took out my neglected school work.

I was just getting down to the correction of such sentences as, 'My granny never had none neither,' when I heard someone at the front door again.

John must have forgotten something. I put aside my papers, and made my way, cursing silently, to the door.

When I opened it, the light fell upon a wispy figure drenched to the skin, with dripping hair and frightened eyes.

'You'd better come in,' I said, following Minnie Pringle into the kitchen.

CHAPTER 9

Minnie Pringle's Problems

Minnie Pringle stood as close as she could to the kitchen heater and dripped steadily from hair, hands and hem-line. If she had just emerged from a river, she could not have been more thoroughly soaked.

'I saw your light,' she said, as if that explained everything.

'I'll get you a towel and something to put on,' I told her. 'Strip off and dump your things in the sink.'

I left her shivering and fumbling with buttons, and went to find underclothes and dressing-gown. When I returned she was sitting on the rush matting on the kitchen floor.

Her back was towards me as she struggled to pull off a wet stocking, and I felt a pang of pity at the sight of her boniness. She might have been a twelve-year-old child, rather than the mother of several children, and pregnant with yet another.

Her normally red hair was now darkly plastered to her head, and dripped down upon her bent back. I noticed dark marks on the shoulders and stick-like upper arms. Could they be bruises? Had Ern really attacked her?

I put the towel round her, and the fresh clothes on the back of the kitchen chair.

'Rub yourself down well,' I said, 'and get dressed. I'm going to make some coffee for us both.'

To the accompaniment of sniffs behind me as Minnie set about her toilet, I busied myself preparing a ham sandwich for my guest. The sink was slowly filling up with sodden garments as we worked, and my head was buzzing with conjectures.

What could have happened? Why had she come to me? Usually, in times of domestic crisis she went to her mother at Springbourne or to her aunt Mrs Pringle at Fairacre. Why me this time?

And what on earth was I to do about her? Obviously, she would have to stay the night, and as luck would have it, the spare bed was made up. As soon as I had made the coffee I would fill a hot-water bottle, but the first thing was to get this poor drowned rat dry, and sitting by my fire with a hot drink.

Within ten minutes we were studying each other before the blazing hearth in my sitting-room. Minnie's teeth still chattered, but she looked pinker than on her arrival, and her hair blazed as brightly as the fire.

I began a little questioning as she grew more relaxed.

'I run off. Ern was real rough this time,' she volunteered.

'But what about the children?'

'My mum's got 'em.'

'Couldn't you have stayed with them?'

She considered this for a moment. 'She never wanted me. She said to go back to Ern. She said my place was with him, but I ain't going back. He knocked me about terrible this time.'

It sounded as though 'being knocked about' was a regular and accepted part of Minnie's marital condition. This time, obviously, Ern had gone beyond the limits of matrimonial behaviour.

'Did you come straight here?'

She looked shocked. 'Oh no! I never wanted to push meself in, like. I went to Auntie's.'

'Mrs Pringle?'

'That's right. But it's her Mothers' Union night, and there wasn't no one there. Uncle Fred was out somewhere too. It was all dark. So I come on here.'

This meant that she had been out in the downpour for the best part of two hours, roaming at least five or six miles in the darkness. I think I was more appalled than she was. This poor little pregnant waif really raised some problems, as well as pity.

She was obviously physically exhausted, although she seemed as usual mentally. She was also ravenously hungry, and I returned to the kitchen to refill her cup and to make a second sandwich. I was seriously perturbed about the possibility of a miscarriage.

My medical skills are sketchy at the best of times, and coping with anything in the gynaecological line would certainly be beyond me. I resolutely put such a possibility from my mind, as I carved ham.

But someone really should be told where she was. I imagined that Ern, poor husband though he was, should be informed, but I knew there was no telephone in Minnie's house. Nor was there in her mother's, nor at Mrs Pringle's.

Minnie was dozing when I returned, but roused herself and attacked the second sandwich with energy.

Half an hour later she was asleep in my spare bed. I washed out the threadbare clothes in the sink, draped them on the clothes horse in front of the fire, and tottered to bed myself.

It was some time before I fell asleep. How to help Minnie was my main concern. It did not seem right to bother her doctor. Ern had been visited by the police before, and I wondered if I should ask for their help again. They had enough to worry them, I decided, with real crime at its present rate, without concerning themselves with this type of domestic upset.

On the other hand, it was obviously unthinkable to send Minnie back to Ern's vicious attacks. In the end, I decided that I must consult Mrs Pringle as soon as I saw her next morning, and meanwhile Minnie must have the sanctuary of my cottage.

*

It dawned on me in the morning that this was Wednesday, and Mrs Pringle would be doing her domestic duties at my home. She and Minnie could get together about future plans during the afternoon.

I left Minnie in bed with a tray of breakfast and strict instructions to stay indoors until her aunt arrived. She seemed to understand, and I set off for school.

'So that's where she got to!' exclaimed Mrs Pringle when I unfolded my tale. 'Ern was at his wits' end when he turned up at his mother's.'

'At his mother's?' I echoed, thoroughly bewildered. How on earth could Mrs Pringle have met Ern's mother anyway, during the rainstorm which had kept most of us indoors last evening?

'We had a real big service of the Mothers' Union at Caxley parish church. Beautiful singing, and the sausage rolls afterwards fairly melted in your mouth.'

'And Ern's mother was there?'

'Yes. She's always been a good member in the Caxley branch. Never misses a meeting, despite the shop.'

I was beginning to get lost again, but Mrs Pringle explained that Ern's mother, when a girl, had been in good service south of Caxley, and had been left a sizeable amount of money by her appreciative employer. This she had wisely invested some years ago in a little corner shop which continued to thrive.

Ern hoped to inherit it eventually, but had proved such an unsatisfactory son to his upright widowed mother, that she was having second thoughts.

'She told Ern so straight. She's always kept a good hold on Ern, and don't hesitate to put him right when he does wrong.'

'Will he take notice of her?'

'That he will!' said Mrs Pringle grimly. 'She give him a

taste of her tongue last night evidently, and she's going over tonight to sort things out. I told her I'd do the same with Minnie when she turned up.'

I was much relieved, and said so. I also told her that I had wondered who to turn to for help.

'Ern's mother and I can cope with this, don't you worry,' she said, heaving herself from the front desk where she had rested her bulk. 'I said to Ern's mother, "Well, here we are at a Mothers' Union meeting, and us mothers should stand together." I know our Minnie isn't much of a mother, but she is one after all.'

She plodded off to the lobby, and I heard the sound of children entering.

I returned to my own duties with feelings of unusual gratitude to my old adversary.

When I arrived again at my Beech Green home, I found that Mrs Pringle had ironed Minnie's outfit, and the kettle was ready for our cups of tea.

Minnie looked much healthier after her night's sleep, and remarkably clean in her newly laundered clothes. I looked out a scarlet cardigan, destined originally for the next jumble sale, to augment her flimsy attire, and though it clashed horribly with her sandy hair, this was no time to worry about sartorial detail, I felt.

Mrs Pringle had obviously given the girl the promised 'talking to', and our drive back to Fairacre was unusually silent. It was a relief to drop them, and to return to the peace of my own home, and the papers I had neglected the evening before.

What, I wondered, as I prised Pussi-luv from the tin for Tibby's supper, would happen when Ern and Minnie met again?

*

The end of term was not far off, and I seemed to have done very little. The children were always somewhat under par at this time of year. Illness had kept several away. The weather had not helped, and we all looked forward to a warm spring and summer to refresh us in body and spirit.

There was one particular event in the future which gave us all some cheer. Henry Mawne had suggested another trip to the Cotswold falconry, and then a visit, that same day, to the Cotswold Wildlife Park near Burford.

Now that our numbers had risen, thanks to the arrival of the two new families, it would be necessary to hire a single-decker bus, and this meant that we could also take several parents who would act as assistants to Mrs Richards and me.

Our earlier visit to the falconry had been paid for by Henry Mawne, and very grateful we were to him. On this occasion, it was only because he knew the staff well that we were able to visit privately and have the complete attention of the people there.

Henry and I worked out the cost per child or adult, and the result was relayed to the children. Of course, they all wanted to go. I sent a note to each household explaining the conditions, time and price, and the response was almost unanimous.

The only children who were not on the list were the three Cotton children. I was surprised at this. Alice had been the keenest child to come when the outing was first mooted, and the two boys seemed equally excited at the idea. Even the Coggs' children were coming, paid for, I suspected, by the vicar. It was puzzling.

Perhaps the Cotton parents did not approve of outings, even educational ones, during school hours? Perhaps their children were travel-sick? Perhaps the family was short of money? Whatever the reason, I did not feel that I could enquire too closely, although I was sorry that the three children would not be among those going.

It was Mrs Pringle who threw some light on the affair.

'Mr Lamb's in a bit of a taking about them Cottons. Don't like to be hard on a family, but he's given 'em a lot of credit, and they don't seem to be making much effort to pay their debts.'

I made no comment. It was easy for Mrs Pringle — or anyone else in the village, for that matter — to start a hefty scandal with the words, 'Miss Read was saying'. You get remarkably canny when you live in a village and 'Least said, soonest mended' is the best motto.

Nevertheless, this snippet, whether true or not, gave me plenty to think about, and I became more alert to the problems of the Cotton children in my care.

About a week before the great day out, Henry arrived at school one afternoon in a state of anxiety.

'Can we fit in one more on the bus?'

I assured him that we could.

'It's my wife's cousin. A nice enough woman, but never gives one any notice. Rang up last night to say she was coming over from Ireland and would stay indefinitely. It's thrown my housekeeper into a panic, I can tell you.'

I could well believe it. Anyone proposing to stay indefinitely, when uninvited anyway, must pose a few household problems.

'You don't think she means to stay *permanently* when she says *indefinitely*?'

'Heaven alone knows! She is what one calls fey. All rather Celtic-twilight and gauzy scarves round the head. Very clever though. Paints very well, and helps at the Abbey Theatre sometimes. But quite unpredictable.' He sighed gustily. 'Anyway, that's one day arranged. I must try to think up further entertainment.'

'Would you like to bring her to tea one day? A Saturday or Sunday would suit me best.'

His face lit up. 'Wonderful! I know she'd like that. I've told her all about you, and she is very keen to meet you.'

'I'll ring you when I get home,' I promised, 'and we'll arrange something.'

He departed looking positively jaunty.

And what, I wondered, had he said to this Irish lady when he had told her 'all about me'?

I looked forward to our meeting with considerable interest, but touched with a little trepidation.

To my surprise, Mrs Pringle returned my ancient red cardigan which I thought I had given to Minnie on that much-disturbed night.

It was freshly laundered, and looked so spruce I seriously thought of keeping it for myself after all.

'Our Minnie,' said Mrs Pringle, 'has settled down again quite nice with Ern, thanks to his mum.'

'I expect you helped too,' I said magnanimously, 'by talking to Minnie.'

'Hardly. Goes in one ear and out the other, with that girl. Nothing between her ears to stop any advice staying in her head. No, give credit where it's due, Ern's mother was the one what settled things.'

'How did she manage that?'

'She told him she was changing her will the minute she heard about any more upsets. He's banking on getting his hands on that shop of hers, and her savings. That really shook him, she said.'

I said that covetousness occasionally had its advantages.

'Mind you,' went on Mrs Pringle, ignoring my comment, 'she's made him go to the doctor too.'

'What's the matter with him?'

Mrs Pringle buttoned up her mouth, and I guessed that I should be denied full knowledge of Ern's visit to the doctor.

'It's not the sort of thing a single lady like you should know about,' she said primly. 'It's to do with Married Life and a Man's Urges.'

'In that case,' I responded, 'I'm sure you are right to say little. But did he really see the doctor?'

Mrs Pringle looked affronted. 'Ern's mother would never had said he did, if he didn't have,' she stated flatly. This sounded the sort of sentence with which I continually grappled, but I did not propose to go into that now.

'Ern's mother is the soul of truth. Lives by the Ten Commandments and signed the pledge too. If she said Ern went to the doctor, then he done just that.'

I apologised for my doubts.

'No offence meant and none taken,' she said graciously. 'Anyway the top and bottom of it is that Minnie shouldn't be put in the family way again, after the present little stranger comes to light.'

'I'm glad to hear it. She has quite enough children as it is.'

Mrs Pringle began to move towards the door.

'Well, we'll just have to see,' she replied gloomily. 'You can't take anything Minnie does for granted. After all, Ern isn't the only man in her life. It makes you think, don't it? You be thankful you're single, Miss Read.'

'I am,' I told her.

The proposed tea party took place on the following Sunday, and Amy had come over to help with my entertaining.

James was away on yet another business trip, and Amy said that she could not wait to meet a fey Irishwoman in gauze scarves.

In actual fact, Deirdre Lynch was dressed in a particularly smart purple outfit with amethysts to match, and Amy and I looked positively dowdy in contrast.

Henry was in buoyant spirits, and inclined to be rather facetious.

'I told you what a ray of sunshine Miss Read has been,' he said to Deirdre. 'I don't know what I should have done without her to guide me through the darkness.'

She smiled vaguely, not appearing to hear half that was said, and I wondered if she were deaf perhaps.

She contributed little to the conversation, until Amy mentioned some Irish friends. Evidently they were neighbours, and our visitor became more animated.

'Not that I go out much now,' she said. 'So many little upsets, you know. Our local pub was bombed last week, and four people blown up.'

Some little upset, was my private thought!

'That's why I am beginning to wonder about coming to live over here.'

Henry, startled, dropped a piece of cake on the floor, and bent to retrieve it. His face was pink when he returned to an upright position, but whether with shock or stooping, it was impossible to say.

'What! Permanently?' he spluttered.

'It seems a good idea. I have lots of friends here – you included, Henry dear – and I think a cottage just like this one would be a perfect place to live.'

Henry began to look very unhappy, and champed his cake moodily.

'I thought I could stay with you while I looked around,' continued Deirdre. She turned to me.

'Do you know of anything?'

'Not at the moment.'

Amy came to the rescue with her usual aplomb. 'Why not get *The Caxley Chronicle* while you are over here? Always lots of houses for sale. And we've some very reliable estate agents in this area. I'm sure you would find something.'

Henry choked, and gave a malevolent look in Amy's direction.

'I don't think it will be convenient for you to stay with me,' he said, when he had regained his breath. 'I'm particularly busy over Easter. This egg hunt, you know, for the children. You are giving me a hand with that, aren't you?'

He turned an appealing face to me. I felt a twinge of guilt.

'We are going away together,' put in Amy quickly. 'We shall be in Shropshire for a few days over the Easter weekend.'

Henry looked stricken. 'But I was *relying* on you,' he wailed. 'I don't think I can manage without your help.'

Deirdre looked smug. 'I shall be there to help, Henry. I don't plan to return to Ireland for some time yet.'

'More tea?' I enquired brightly.

'I believe a robin is looking for a nesting place in my garden,' said Amy, backing me up in my rescue attempt.

Henry continued to look furious. 'Too early,' he said tersely.

When they had departed, Amy lit a cigarette, and sank back on the sofa with a sigh.

'Well, what a to-do. That man is heavily smitten with you, my love, and you'll have to do something about it. If I know anything about these affairs, our Deirdre has got her eye on him, and he knows it. You'll have to come to his rescue. You could do much worse. He's a very nice fellow, I've always thought, and absolutely devoted to you.'

'Oh, shut up, Amy!' I snapped. 'Henry must fight his own battles. I'm not taking him on.'

Amy laughed so heartily that I was forced to join in.

'Let's get out the map and plan our route to Bridgnorth,' she suggested. 'It's time you had a break, I can see.'

'Hear, hear!' I agreed warmly.

Two days before we broke up for the Easter holidays, the trip to the Cotswolds took place in perfect weather.

The stone villages glowed warmly in the spring sunshine and every now and then we crossed the River Windrush, with the willows drooping freshly green branches above it.

Most of the children were already acquainted with the birds of prey and their attendants and all were greeted as old friends. There was no shortage of volunteers to offer arms as perches to the great birds as they showed off their capabilities.

The Cotswold Wildlife Park was enjoyed with equal enthusiasm by the children, but my pleasure was somewhat marred by Henry's behaviour.

As soon as we took our places in the bus, Henry sat beside me. Deirdre sat in the seat behind, and occasionally leant forward to speak to him. He was not very forthcoming to Deirdre's comments, but talked brightly to me, virtually ignoring his visitor.

At the first opportunity, I changed my place, making sure that I was adequately hemmed in by children. When we stopped, however, to go round the falconry or the park, Henry appeared at my side. So, I noticed, did Deirdre.

I escaped every now and again, excusing myself saying

that the children needed attention. It was all rather irritating, and done, I felt sure, to annoy Deirdre in which, I was glad to see, he did not succeed.

She stayed close to Henry throughout, and on this occasion was actually wearing one of the gauzy scarves draped attractively round her head. I was getting rather fond of Deirdre, I decided, looking across the eagles' enclosure where I had found temporary sanctuary.

She was obviously good-tempered, impervious to Henry's rudeness, and implacably intent on winning him with her charms.

And good luck to her, I thought. Perhaps, by the time I returned from my break with Amy and James, she would have succeeded.

What a relief that would be!

CHAPTER 10

Romantic Complications

I was particularly glad to welcome the Easter holidays. Although I could not complain of anything definite about my health, and managed, I thought, to perform my duties as well as ever, I was conscious of being a little below par.

For one thing, I did not sleep as soundly as I had before my strokes, and I tired more quickly if I undertook gardening or furniture shifting. However, I still enjoyed my meals and my walks around the fields and lanes of Fairacre and Beech Green, and reckoned that I was in pretty good shape.

Nevertheless, it would be good to get away. When one is at home there are innumerable little jobs waiting to be done, and out of sight would be out of mind, thank goodness. The bookshelves that needed a thorough cleaning, the curtain linings that needed shortening, the refrigerator that needed defrosting and the bathroom tap that dripped steadily could all be left behind while I kicked up my heels with Amy.

And besides these domestic annoyances there were more personal irritants. Henry Mawne was one, Minnie Pringle's unsatisfactory marriage was another. The unexplained tension among the Cottons was another. It would be a real relief to leave all these problems behind me for a day or two.

On the last day of term Mrs Pringle dropped a plate on the lobby floor, and was unusually upset by this misfortune.

'There! That's the third,' she exclaimed crossly. 'Yesterday it was a pudding basin, and before I come along here today the handle of one of my best cups come away in my hand.'

She stooped to retrieve the pieces.

'My aunt gave it to me years ago,' she went on, red in the face from her exertions. 'A beautiful tea set it was too, though the teapot lid went to glory years ago, and there's only four cups left, but you have to expect that with a teaset over the years.'

I said that there was no need to worry about the school plate. I would re-imburse the kitchen department and explain the matter.

She looked a little more cheerful. 'Well, there's an end to it now, I daresay, as the three's done.'

'The three?'

'Everything always goes in threes. Like three blind mice, and three-in-one-and-one-in-three.'

I felt that mice and the Trinity were in strange juxtaposition in this theory, but forbore to comment.

'Like your strokes,' she continued. 'You've had two, and I'll wager – if I were a betting woman that is – that you'll get a third.'

'Well, really —' I began indignantly, but was ignored.

'Always in *threes*,' repeated the old harpy. 'It was the third as took off my Uncle Ebeneezer in the end. You want to watch out.'

She was out of the door before I could think of a suitable response.

As usual, she had had the last word.

That evening, as I was busy ironing some clothes before

packing them for the holiday, a shadow fell across the ironing board, and there was John Jenkins making his way to the back door.

'Oh, I see you're busy,' he exclaimed.

'Nothing urgent,' I assured him. 'Do come in.'

We went through to the sitting-room, and John settled down as though he intended to stay some time.

He refused tea, coffee, sherry and whisky, and looked about him very happily.

'I was just passing, you know, and I realised I wasn't sure what date we'd fixed for you to see my cottage. What about this weekend?'

I explained that I should be away.

'Pity. I've invited Henry and his girlfriend to supper. He seems in a bit of a tizzy about his visitor. I thought she seemed rather a good sort.'

'So did I.'

He appeared surprised. 'Did you now? I think Henry felt you might be upset. He said as much to me. Out of Deirdre's hearing, of course.'

I began to feel my usual irritation with Henry's behaviour, but managed to answer equably. 'I've no idea why Henry should imagine that I mind at all,' I said.

'He's very fond of you,' said John. 'Understandably.'

He looked at me with such a strange expression on his face that I felt alarm overtaking my irritation. Not *another* suitor? How delighted Amy would be!

'I'm sorry about this weekend,' I replied briskly. 'Could we arrange another day? I'll get my diary.'

I had left it upstairs, and although I was glad of a few minutes' respite from John's company, I was not best pleased to discover Tibby stretched out asleep on the eiderdown with a headless mouse alongside.

I snatched up my diary, left the two to get on with it,

and returned to find John leaning on the mantelpiece in a dejected manner.

'I could come on Thursday or Friday of next week,' I offered. He appeared to rally slightly.

'Not Thursday. I'm expecting a new fellow to start on the garden that day, and I ought to oversee him.'

'You're lucky! How did you get him? Jobbing gardeners are thin on the ground these days.'

'I put a postcard in Fairacre Post Office. This man called the same day.'

'Do I know him?'

'He's called Arthur Coggs.'

'Oh lor'! Our Arthur!'

'So you know him?'

'Everyone knows Arthur round here. You'll have to watch him if he does turn up, which I doubt. He's the local ne'er-do-well.'

John looked grim. I found it preferable to the amorous glance he had earlier given me.

'I didn't think he looked very prepossessing, I must admit, but I thought I'd give him a try.'

'Why not?'

John sat down again, just as I had thought he was about to go.

'This is where you are such a help,' he remarked. 'You seem to know everybody.'

'Well, I ought to. I taught most of them over the years.'

'I suppose it is just being a newcomer in such a tight little community, but I must admit that I feel very lonely at times. The complete outsider.'

'You'll soon make lots of friends,' I said bracingly. 'What about Friday then?'

I held up my diary.

'Friday. That will be fine.'

He stood up, and held out his hand, which I obligingly took to shake, but was dismayed to find that he did not relinquish mine.

'You were my first friend here,' he said. 'I shall never forget it.'

I thought that I could smell scorching coming from the kitchen. For pity's sake, had I left the iron switched on? I could not tug the poor fellow willy-nilly along to see, but I wished he would let go of my hand of his own volition.

'John,' I said very kindly, I hope, 'I'm as pleased as you are to be friends, and I look forward to seeing the cottage on Friday week.'

At that he let go of my hand and gave me a wonderful smile. No doubt about it, he was a very handsome man.

I let him out of the front door. I certainly felt affectionate towards John Jenkins and wanted to see him again.

Meanwhile, the matters in my kitchen and bedroom needed more immediate attention, and any tender emotions must take second place.

It was good to be heading north-west to Shropshire on the afternoon of Good Friday.

We skirted most towns, but the few that we went through seemed busy.

Amy was rather censorious. 'In my young days,' she said, 'everything shut down on Good Friday. Even the level crossing near our home was closed.'

'You're thinking of footpaths,' James told her.

Amy wrinkled her brow. 'Well, perhaps I was,' she conceded, 'but the point is that Good Friday was really *observed*. Now you can pop into any shop for a pound of tea or a quarter of lamb's liver whenever you like.'

'The other way round,' commented James, jamming on the brakes to let a pheasant stroll haughtily across the road. 'You'd never buy a *pound* of tea at a time!'

'And talking of tea,' said Amy, quite unruffled, 'let's stop soon and have a cup somewhere.'

On this, we were all in agreement.

The hotel, when we arrived at around six o'clock, was all we had hoped. It was a solidly built house which had once been a Victorian vicarage, with a pleasant grassy garden and mature trees. The coach house and stables had been turned into attractive rooms, and other additions, such as a large sun room, blended well with the original building.

James dropped us off in Bridgnorth the next day while he visited his business friend, and Amy and I pottered about shopping, and found the funicular railway which descended from the town centre down the steep drop to the side of the River Severn.

We spent the day exploring until James picked us up again as arranged, at about six, in a car park near by.

'I feel as though I've been on the beach all day,' said Amy happily. 'All blown about in the freshest of fresh air.'

It was later that evening when James enquired after the new families at Fairacre, and I had a chance to tell him about the odd behaviour of Mrs Cotton.

He looked grave. 'I can't understand this. There should be no shortage of money. The Trust is very generous, and the whole point of the exercise is to give the children a happy home with the usual little treats such as your school outing.'

'I know. That's what's so odd. They don't live extravagantly, and I don't think he's a betting man. He certainly doesn't waste his money at the pub. Bob Willet told me that.'

'Bob Willet? Is he the local tippler?'

'Far from it! You're mixing him up with Arthur Coggs. Bob is an upright and God-fearing teetotaller, and Mrs Willet keeps him that way. He is also my chief informant on village affairs.'

'So what's his opinion?'

'He's as puzzled as I am, I think, though I haven't really discussed the matter much with him.'

James rubbed his chin thoughtfully. 'I'll call one day soon,' he promised. He must have seen my look of alarm. 'Don't worry. You won't be mentioned. It'll be a casual dropping-in to see how things are going. It's quite usual for a member of the board to keep a friendly eye on such matters.'

I went to bed with mixed feelings. Was I being meddlesome in the Cotton family's affairs? Should I have told James about my fears which were possibly groundless?

On the other hand, it was good to have James's support, and if there were troubles in that household he was the ideal man to put them right.

I did not worry for long. Good Shropshire air ensured that I slept soundly for eight hours.

We returned by a different route, travelling through the border country between England and Wales, more beautiful than ever with the trees decked in their spring finery. Here and there the wild cherries were in early bloom, reminding me of Housman's poem:

> *Loveliest of trees, the cherry now*
> *Is hung with bloom along the bough,*
> *And stands about the woodland ride*
> *Wearing white for Eastertide.*

In my Beech Green garden the daffodils were beginning to break, and there was the scent of spring everywhere.

The cottage was clean from Mrs Pringle's ministrations, and Tibby greeted me with unusual enthusiasm.

Altogether, it was good to be back, and the thought of almost a fortnight of the school holidays still stretching before me was an added bonus.

It was odd to realise that this holiday was the last one before a term. At the end of the summer term I should be at the outset of my retirement.

I contemplated the matter. Did it alarm me? Did I feel apprehensive about changing my way of life for – who knows? Twenty years of pleasing myself? Of going where I wanted when I wanted? Should I get fed up with my own company? Should I feel that life was aimless without the discipline and structure of a school year which had shaped everything for me for so long?

I had now had several months to get used to the idea, and it was a considerable relief to find that I now looked forward with enormous pleasure to the years ahead.

On Friday afternoon I put on my new cardigan suit and set off to have tea with John Jenkins.

On my way I saw my first butterfly of the season and noticed that the hawthorn hedges were beginning to break into leaf. Lambs skittered about Hundred Acre field on my left, and the sun was warm. I felt in high spirits.

John's cottage stood back from the narrow road we all call Pig Lane. It must have once been built of brick and flint, as mine is, and so many local cottages are. But some earlier inhabitant had lime-washed it, and the effect was very fresh and pleasing, although the purists might regret the concealment of interesting native brickwork.

It was somewhat larger than mine, and John had added an elegant conservatory at the rear. This led from his sitting-room, and gave a feeling of light and space.

Upstairs there were three bedrooms, larger and loftier than my own, and certainly lighter. I congratulated him on having found such an attractive place.

'My friends say it's really too big, but I need at least one spare bedroom for visitors, and in any case I'm used to big houses. I was brought up in a vast Victorian villa complete with a basement and attics. We must have had over sixty stairs.'

I followed him into the kitchen, and was impressed with the competence with which he dealt with setting out the tray and coping with the kettle and teapot, and all the other trappings.

'I don't rise to making my own scones yet,' he said, offering me the dish when we had settled by the fire. 'I get these from Lamb at the Post Office.'

This reminded me of the postcard he had put up, and I enquired about Arthur.

'Well, he turned up. I set him to cutting back a patch of scrub at the end of the garden, and he seemed to make some headway. I think I'll give him a trial run.'

'Watch your tools then,' I warned him, 'or anything else he can put in his pocket. Our Arthur needs a lot of beer, and he has to make a bit of money on the side for that.'

He said that he would be vigilant, and went on to enquire about my holiday.

I waxed enthusiastic about Bridgnorth and the country around it, and told him about a veteran car museum that James had taken us to, and about the ancient but glittering Lagonda I had fallen for.

'That's the sort of thing I miss,' he said, when I had run out of breath. 'The companionship and the fun of shared outings.'

'But you have made friends here,' I said, 'and you know Henry from the old days.'

'A little of Henry's company goes a long way,' he said. 'He can be very tiresome at times.'

I felt sorry that I had mentioned Henry. I had no wish to make mischief, but surely the two men were not vying for my favours? It was an uncomfortable thought.

I was soon enlightened.

'It would be very kind of you to agree to accompany me now and again on a little expedition. You know that I relish your company, and I should appreciate it so much.'

One cannot very well say, 'As long as the relationship remains friendly and not romantic', but that was in my thoughts.

Aloud I said that I should enjoy an outing with him now and again, although the next term would keep me unusually busy while it lasted.

'But then you'll be retired,' he said eagerly, 'and have time on your hands. You are bound to feel a little lost – even lonely – when you first retire.'

I did not like to point out that I had never yet been lonely in my life as a single woman, that I enjoyed my own company, and that I was looking forward to many hours of solitude. He might feel that I was criticising his own recent feelings, and I did not want to appear censorious. Luckily, he turned to another subject.

'I'm thinking of getting a dog. I thought of the Caxley Dog Rescue place. Do you know anything about it?'

'Not personally, but I'll consult Bob Willet. He'll know.'

The Easter holidays flew by at their usual surprising speed, and I was left contemplating all those jobs I had been going to tackle, and had not.

The curtain linings still remained unshortened, and the bookshelves uncleaned, but the bath tap had had a new washer and the refrigerator had been defrosted. I told myself that half the jobs had been tackled, and that was a better record than some of my school-holiday schedules.

As was usual, the first day of term dawned sunny and clear, and I thought how lovely it would be to potter about in the garden with the birds fluttering about collecting food for their nestlings, and to enjoy the scent of spring flowers. However, duty called, and I set off to face my last term at Fairacre school.

Mrs Pringle's leg must have 'flared up' again, as I noticed that she was limping about her dusting routine, a sure sign of trouble. What dire happening was I to hear of now, I wondered?

'I'm off to the doctor this evening,' said Mrs Pringle. 'I was knocked down by that Arthur Coggs.'

'Good heavens! How was that?'

'I went out late last night to put a birthday card in Lamb's letter box to catch first post this morning. It's my Auntie Margaret's eightieth tomorrow, and I want her to know I've remembered her. I'm in her will.'

'So how did you meet Arthur?'

'He was stepping out – or rather, *falling out* – of the Beetle and Wedge, and he was in a real drunken state. He bumped into me, and it's a wonder I didn't fall to the ground and break a hip. What's more, he never said a word of apology! Jogged my bad leg something cruel.'

I rendered my sympathy.

'That Arthur Coggs has been too flush with money lately for his own good. I date it from when he started work at that friend of yours up Pig Lane. He must be paying him over the odds. Everyone's talking about it.'

I felt some alarm. Could John have left valuables about despite my warning? Perhaps I should make enquiries when I returned home? Or was this none of my business?

Ernest appeared at the door.

'Can I ring the bell, miss? You never said nothing about who could.'

Clearly John Jenkins' affairs must wait. School affairs now engulfed me, including my old enemy, the double negative.

As it happened, John rang me as soon as I returned home.

He had been invited to the book launch of a local writer and would I accompany him?

As it was the same evening as our Parents' Association meeting at the school I was obliged to decline, but I was sorry. It certainly sounded more fun. However, duty came first.

I decided to broach the subject of Arthur's temporary affluence.

'You haven't missed anything?'

'No. Though I haven't looked thoroughly. Should I?'

'It wouldn't be a bad idea. Do you keep any money about? It sounded as though he had paper money.'

'Hang on. I'll have a quick look.'

I waited, stroking Tibby, who was impatient for a snack.

John sounded breathless when he returned. 'You're right! Two ten-pound notes missing from my desk drawer. I keep a hundred stashed there for any emergency.'

'When did you look last?'

'Can't say. I notice them, of course, when I go to get stamps and so on from the drawer, but if it looks undisturbed I naturally think the hundred is still there. What a fool I am! I should have thought of this.'

He sounded very put out, as well he might be.

'But does Arthur ever come inside your house?'

'I've shown him where the lavatory is in case he needs it.'

'And he'd pass the desk?'

'No, but the door is always open into the sitting-room. The desk's in full view of the hall.'

'Unlocked?'

'Not now it won't be,' he said grimly. 'I shall tackle him about it, but I don't know if it's a police affair. I should have been more careful.'

I felt very sorry for him. 'Cheer up!' I said. 'At least you know more about our Arthur Coggs.'

He gave a snort of disgust. 'And about myself too, alas!'

PART THREE

SUMMER TERM

CHAPTER 11

Something Unexpected

The first week of my last term as a school mistress was one of unbroken sunshine unusual for April.

The early mornings were particularly idyllic. In my garden the daffodils flourished their golden trumpets, and sturdy double tulips glowed in a stone trough by my front door. The lilac bushes bore pyramids of blue-grey buds, ready to burst into fragrant bloom, and everywhere the small birds darted feverishly in their search for food for their young.

The drive along the leafy lane to Fairacre was equally enchanting. The blackthorn bushes were a froth of white blossom which spilled into the road with every gust of wind, strewing the surface with petal-confetti. Lambs gambolled in the fields, larks sang above and it was almost too much to ask to go into school on such mornings.

I comforted myself with the exquisite thought that by next spring time I should be able to revel freely in all this feverish excitement of flora and fauna, untouched by the stern finger of duty pointing me to a bleaker path.

Now that the end of my professional life was so near I looked forward to freedom with ever-increasing pleasure. I even began to wonder why I had not given up years ago.

'Because you would have starved,' rebuked my sensible half.

'But think of the fun you've missed,' pointed out my frivolous half.

'Never mind,' I told myself, swinging the car into the school playground. 'It's all waiting for me at the end of term.'

One such blissful morning I was on playground duty when Eve Umbleditch emerged from my old home and joined me.

'What a day!' she said, turning her face up to the cloudless sky.

'Too good to work,' I agreed.

'Not for much longer, though. I came to ask you to supper one evening soon.'

I said I should love to come.

'Now that Andrew's a better sleeper, we feel we can do a little evening entertaining. What about next Wednesday?'

I promised to confirm this when I got home to my diary, and found it was then time to usher my charges back to school.

Later that day I rang Eve to say how much I looked forward to the party at Fairacre school house, as it once was, in my time.

'Good! We've asked John Jenkins as well. He was at the same school as Horace. Isn't it a small world?'

I agreed that it was indeed.

'And the Bakers. Gerard and Miriam,' continued Eve. 'Just the six of us. Anyway, as you know only too well, the dining-room won't hold any more.'

'It's the perfect number,' I assured her.

'I expect John will bring you,' she added. 'Unless you like to pick him up as you pass Pig Lane.'

'We'll fix something,' I promised, and rang off.

Almost immediately it rang again. It was John Jenkins.

'I hear we've been invited to the Umbleditches. What time shall I call for you?'

'Well, actually I had thought of picking you up, as I shall be coming your way.'

'No, no! Wouldn't hear of it. *I* shall collect *you*. It will make my day to have you to myself for a little time.'

'That's kind of you. Shall we say six thirty here?'

And so it was settled.

I pottered about the garden doing a little perfunctory weeding until it grew dark, and I went indoors.

My thoughts turned upon this new friend John Jenkins. There was no deluding myself. The man was getting remarkably attentive, and I should have to make up my mind what to do about it.

Here he was, in the same vulnerable state as Henry Mawne, a lone man obviously in need of companionship. Was I willing to supply it?

Occasionally, yes, was my reply to this self-posed query, but not on any permanent basis. He was an attractive man, he could offer a woman good company, protection and a comfortable home, and many a lone female, I felt sure, would be happy to consider marriage. However, I was not.

As Amy had so often pointed out, I was far too fond of my own company. Further, she was wont to add, I was very selfish, and it would do me good to have to consider someone else in my life. Look how much richer her own life was, she would say, married to James!

I forbore on these occasions to remind her of her unhappiness when James was away, presumably on business but, I guessed, with some dalliance with other ladies thrown in. Amy was no fool, and knew better than I did, I suspected, about such matters, but she was rock-bottom loyal, and never breathed a word about her doubts.

She was probably right about my selfishness, but what was wrong with that? I coped with my own worries as well as my own pleasures, without embroiling anyone else in my affairs. I gave help to others whenever I could, as in the case of poor distracted Minnie, and I suppose I could have done a great deal more if I had joined such excellent bodies as the Red Cross or the Samaritans, but I was never one for joining things, and in any case my spare time was limited.

No, the fact of the matter was that single life suited me admirably, and now that I was in my comfortable middle age I was decidedly set in my ways and would very much dislike sharing my home with someone else. There was a lot to be said for a lone existence, and I recalled a remark of Katherine Mansfield's when she said, 'If you find a hair in your honey, at least you know it's your own.'

I only hoped that John Jenkins' ardour would cool, and that Deirdre would be successful in capturing my other, rather less troublesome, admirer.

One could quite see the attractions of the monastic life, I thought, prising Pussi-luv out of the tin.

Promptly at six thirty on the following Wednesday, John's car arrived. He must have spent hours polishing it. It gleamed from nose to tail, and put my own shabby runabout to shame.

The evening was overcast but warm, and the heady scents of spring were all around.

John was cheerful, and not too embarrassingly solicitous, and my spirits rose as we approached my old home.

'Do you miss it?' he asked as we drew up.

'Not really. I think I prefer the cottage at Beech Green. For one thing, it is full of happy memories of Dolly Clare, and it is my own. This was only lent to me for the duration of my working life. I was always very conscious of that.'

'You are like me. I like to feel settled.'

Luckily, at this juncture, Horace appeared and greeted us. Soon the two men were reminiscing about their old school and the idiosyncrasies of some of the staff they remembered.

It was good to see Miriam and Gerard again. He was in the throes of producing a television series about diarists, and we all gave him conflicting and confused ideas about the people he should put in. I plumped for Parson Woodforde and Francis Kilvert. Miriam said John Evelyn was absolutely essential. Eve said that Gerard could do a whole series on Samuel Pepys alone, and we all got extremely excited about the project and bombarded poor Gerard with our ideas.

He bore it all very well, and when we had run out of breath, said mildly that he was not going to use any of those diarists but some unknown Dorset individuals he had come across when reading about various seventeenth-century writers.

John, with considerable aplomb, changed the subject to gardening while we got over our disappointments and paid more attention to our excellent roast lamb and redcurrant jelly. It was salutory to remember, I told myself, that writers and other creative artists do not relish other people's ideas. They usually have more than enough of their own, and well-meant suggestions only add to the burden of their already over-stocked minds.

Miriam and I were taken to see Andrew asleep upstairs, in my old spare bedroom, once we had finished at the table. He looked so rosy and angelic, with dark crescents of eyelashes against his velvety cheeks, that it was difficult to believe that I had seen him that morning roaring his head off, in a paroxysm of infant rage, when I had been on playground duty.

The rain had swept in whilst we were enjoying ourselves

and by the time we drove back to Beech Green the roads were awash, hard rain spun silver coins on the tarmac and the windscreen wipers were working overtime.

We passed the end of Pig Lane, and we soon approached my cottage.

'Stay there,' commanded John, as we drew up, 'and I'll get an umbrella from the boot.'

Huddled together we made a dash for the front door, John holding the umbrella over me while I found the key.

'You must come in,' I said.

'Thank you,' he replied, scattering showers of raindrops as he closed the umbrella.

'Coffee?' I asked, as he divested himself of his coat.

'How nice.'

I proceeded to the kitchen to do my duties. Frankly, I should have preferred to go to straight to bed, rather than sit making polite conversation, but I reminded myself of the fact that I had been fetched and carried, and protected from the downpour.

The fire was low, but I put on some small logs, much to Tibby's satisfaction, and we sipped our coffee companionably.

'I hope I'm not keeping you from your bed.'

'Not at all,' I said politely, stifling a yawn.

'It's wonderful to be here. So marvellously *cosy*. The fire, you know, and the cat, and you just sitting there.'

I wondered if he would prefer me to stand on my head, or leap about the room in a lively polka, but was too tired to do anything but smile.

'This is what I miss,' he said earnestly. 'The companionship, the sharing of things.'

Not again, I prayed silently. I was really too sleepy to listen sympathetically to any man's description of his loneliness.

He put his cup and saucer very carefully in the hearth, a

move which I viewed with some apprehension. If this was a prelude to a proposal of marriage I must be on my guard. I felt such a longing for my bed that I might well accept him simply to terminate the evening's proceedings, and how should I feel in the morning?

He rose from his armchair and came to sit on a footstool very close to me. The light from the table lamp shone on his silvery hair. He really was an extremely handsome man.

'I'm sure you know how I feel about you,' he began, speaking quickly. 'It began when I first saw you. I had a premonition that we were destined to mean a great deal to each other. Do you feel that too?'

He looked so earnest, and his blue eyes were so pleading that I could quite see how easily I could agree.

'Well, I must say,' I began weakly, but was interrupted, rather rudely I thought, by my hand being snatched up and squeezed somewhat painfully. Aunt Clara's garnet ring was always rather small, and it was now being ground into my finger.

'Don't put me off,' he begged. 'Don't turn me down. You mean so much to me, and I couldn't bear it if you said "No". Say you'll think about it, if you need time. But what I dearly want to hear is that you would marry me.'

It was all said in such a rush, blurted out so urgently that there was no mistaking the sincerity of the offer. I was deeply touched, and withdrew my mangled hand as unobtrusively as I could.

'Dear John,' I began.

'You will?' he cried, attempting to retrieve my hand again. 'You'll have me? Oh, I can't tell you —'

'I didn't say that,' I pointed out. Was I never to get a word in edgeways?

He checked suddenly, and began to look crestfallen.

'Do have your coffee while it's hot,' I said. 'I was about to say, John dear, that I am truly fond of you, and it's wonderful for me to receive a proposal at my age. Let me think it over, may I?'

He sighed, and sat more upright on the footstool. I fetched his coffee and gave it to him.

'I suppose I shall have to be content with "truly fond", but I beg you to take pity on me. I'd do anything for you. We could move to wherever you fancied. Go abroad if you like. To France, say. I've a little cottage there. I'm not a rich man, but we shouldn't want for anything, and I do most dearly love you.'

'I know that. It touches me deeply.'

He put down the coffee cup again. It was still almost full. He stood up, and put his arms round me.

'Say you'll think about it. Say you'll tell me quickly. I shan't have an easy minute until I know. And please, *please* say "Yes".'

He kissed me very gently and made for the door. Outside the rain lashed down more fiercely than ever, and I handed him the umbrella which was still glistening with raindrops.

'I'll ring you tomorrow,' I promised, as he ran down the path.

Within a minute he was off, with a valedictory toot of the horn, and I put the cups and saucers in the sink, and put the fireguard round the ashes of the logs, and put myself, at long last, between the sheets.

What a day! I felt exhausted with all this emotion.

I had plenty to think about the next morning. I looked at myself in the looking-glass and wondered why anyone should want to marry me.

Certainly my hair was still thick and had very little grey in it, and I had always been fortunate enough to have a good skin, but otherwise I was humdrum enough in all conscience.

It was very flattering, though, to receive a proposal of marriage in one's late fifties, and I was duly elated in a moderate and middle-aged way. Perhaps, I thought, with some deflation, John had already asked more attractive women and they had turned him down?

Not with that silvery hair and those devastating blue eyes, I decided. He would make a most decorative adjunct to anyone's household, and no doubt be quite useful too in little manly things like changing electric light bulbs and washers on taps.

But did I want him? The answer was definitely 'No'! A pity, but there it was, and the really wretched thing was that I must tell him so in the kindest possible way.

I drove to school rehearsing different ways of turning down a nice man's proposal of marriage. They all seemed pretty brutal, and I was glad to reach school and to be confronted by my exuberant pupils.

Mrs Richards did not appear, and I took the entire school for prayers in my classroom. It was a quarter past nine when she arrived, full of apologies. Her car was being repaired. Wayne's van would not start. She had been obliged to go to catch the bus, and promised to tell me more at playtime.

Meanwhile, she hastened to her own duties, and I to mine. Every now and again, the awful fact of the impending telephone call I must make plunged me into gloom.

Mrs Pringle, arriving with clean tea towels, commented on my looks. 'Proper peaky again. You want to watch you don't have another funny turn,' she told me.

I said that I felt quite well. I could have said that if I were to have any more funny turns, it was not much good setting out to watch them, but I was in no mood to cross swords with Mrs Pringle in my present debilitated condition, and let it pass.

At playtime Mrs Richards enlarged on her early morning difficulties as we sipped our coffee.

'There I was by the bus stop when Alan came along and gave me a lift. I've known him for years. He was sweet on me at one time, but I was only eighteen and he was quite old, about thirty.'

I thought of John Jenkins, who must be in his sixties. No doubt Mrs Richards would consider him in his dotage. Perhaps he was? A dispiriting thought.

'He was a proper pest,' she went on, 'and I asked my mum to choke him off. She told him I was about to be engaged to Wayne, and I was furious with her.'

'Why?'

'Well, I'd only been out once or twice with Wayne, and I didn't want him to think that I was running after him. I mean, I knew I could never take to Alan. You always know, don't you?'

I agreed fervently that indeed one did always know.

'But I was quite keen on Wayne, and I thought people would tittle-tattle and he'd be frightened off. It was stupid of my mum to say that, wasn't it?'

'I must get out to the playground,' I said, 'before murder is done.'

Out in the fresh air, with the rooks wheeling about the trees, and the children rushing around being aeroplanes or trains, I felt much better.

On the whole, I thought that my assistant had been jolly lucky to have a mother to take her part. If only I had someone to 'choke off' my poor old John!

Well, it would have to be me, and perhaps that was all for the best, I decided, as we returned to the classroom.

It was almost five o'clock when I returned home, as I had been waylaid by a parent who was worried about her child's asthma and wanted to know if PE lessons upset him.

It seemed sensible to fortify myself with a cup of tea before tackling my difficult task. It was a bright afternoon and no doubt John was either in his garden or even farther afield. Would it be better to wait until it became dark, I wondered? He would be much more likely to be near the telephone then.

On the other hand, I wanted to get the job over. Besides, if I rang after six o'clock he might think I had waited for the cheap rate period, and I should appear parsimonious as well as callous. How difficult life is!

I finished my tea, took a deep breath, and rang John's

number. He must have been standing by the telephone, for it only gave two rings.

'Thank God it's you,' he said. 'I've been snatching up the phone all day, and had the laundry, the vicar, George Annett, and some idiot trying to get Venezuela. I've been dying for you to ring.'

'Well, I was at school,' I said weakly.

'Of course! I'd forgotten that.'

'I've only just got in.'

'You poor darling. You must be whacked. You need a cup of tea.'

I did not like to say that I had just had one. It seemed so heartless, especially as he had obviously had a distracting day.

'About last night,' I began, and wondered how to go on. Should I ask him if he remembered asking me to marry him? Should I say that I had been thinking of his kind offer? Should I say that I was feeling terrible? This last was true enough anyway.

Luckily, John took over the initiative.

'You've decided? Is it "Yes" or "No"? Please say it's "Yes"! I can't tell you how much it means to me.'

'John, it has to be "No", I fear.'

There was a strange sound at the other end. A sigh? A sob? A laugh?

He sounded calm when he spoke again.

'I was afraid it would be so. But at least you haven't asked me to be "just a good friend" because I'm a dam' sight more than that.'

'I know, John, and I'm sorry to have to refuse.'

'Well, there it is. No harm done, and I give you fair warning that I shall try again.'

'Please, John —' I said in alarm.

'Don't worry, I shan't pester you, but I'm not giving up.'

'Oh dear!'

'Will you come to a concert with me at Oxford next month?'

'Thank you. I should like that.'

'There's a nice girl! And wear that blue thing you had on last night. It was so pretty.'

He rang off before I could say any more.

Last night? Was it only *last night* that all this had blown up? Thank heaven he had taken it so well. My knees were knocking together after my ordeal, and I tottered into the garden to recover.

It was over anyway, and having staved off his first proposal I felt sure that I could cope with any more to come. Anyway, it would be nice to go to a concert with him later on.

What was it he had said? 'That *blue* thing, that looked so pretty.'

I had always thought it was *green*. Ah well!

CHAPTER 12

Romantic Speculations in Fairacre

Bob Willet was busy doing something to the school gate when I drove into the playground the next morning.

'Dropped a bit,' he explained. 'Them dratted kids swings on it.'

'I know. I've told them not to dozens of times.'

'You wants to give 'em a clip round the earhole.'

'I agree, but I'd probably lose my job these days.'

'Mind you,' went on Mr Willet fairly, 'most gates drop a bit. I had to do Mr Mawne's last week.'

'How is he?'

'Chipper. Very chipper indeed. His lady visitor's gone back to Ireland.'

'He'll be relieved.'

'But she's coming back! It seems she's gone back to put her house on the market.'

'So she is going to settle here after all?'

'Looks like it. And settled in with Mr Mawne if she gets half a chance.'

'Oh dear!'

He gave me a swift look, and I wondered if he expected to see disappointment in my countenance. Or perhaps relief?

'She's a very nice woman,' I said. 'I liked her.'

'But ain't she related to Mr Mawne? I was going to look up the Table of Infinity in my prayer book, but I trimmed the privet hedge instead.'

'She's no relation of Henry's. It was Mrs Mawne who was her cousin.'

Bob Willet looked slightly dejected, and hit the gate a thwacking blow with his hammer.

'Well, I suppose that's fair enough,' he said, 'but I'd sooner see Mr Mawne looking nearer at hand for a good wife.'

At that moment Mrs Pringle arrived, her oil-cloth bag bulging.

'Brought you some early spinach,' she puffed. 'Do you good to get a bit of green down you.'

I expressed my thanks and we left Bob Willet to enter the lobby together.

It was a most generous present, and I could see that most of it would have to go in the freezer for another day.

'Fred put cloches over 'em,' explained Mrs Pringle. 'Brought 'em on a treat. I've given a bag to Minnie, though she says her kids won't eat greens. I said to tell them that thousands of poor children would be thankful for a nice plate of spinach. But you know Minnie. She won't say nothing.'

'And how is she? When's that baby due?'

I suddenly remembered that evening of lashing rain last March when Minnie had sought refuge with me. Surely, I had not seen her since then, and I wondered how her stormy marriage was faring.

'The baby? Oh, that came to nothing,' said Mrs Pringle in an off-hand manner.

She must have seen my astonishment.

'Minnie's always in a muddle with her dates and that, and she thought there was another little stranger on the way. All for the best there wasn't.'

I agreed. It was certainly for the best, both for Minnie and the little stranger, in the present circumstances.

'I hear Mr Mawne's lady has left him at last. She's got her eye on him, you know. Bob Willet told me she's going to come back again.'

'Well, it's a free country,' I said equably.

'Not when you go shopping in Caxley on market day,' said Mrs Pringle. 'Why, I paid nearly a pound for a piece of cheese, that hardly did Fred's supper.'

Her cheeks wobbled with outrage, and reminded me of a flustered turkey-cock.

But at least the subject was changed, and that was a great relief.

Arthur Coggs had appeared in the magistrates' court at Caxley, so the local paper said, on a number of charges of theft.

The chairman had deferred sentence as he said he felt sure that there were some deep-seated problems in Arthur's past, so that the bench needed an up-to-date report from the probation officer and one from a psychiatrist.

Mr Willet was scathing. 'Anyone in Fairacre could tell him what Arthur's deep-seated problem is. He won't work, that's all. And he likes his beer. Put the two together and our Arthur's going to be in trouble all his life.'

He was right of course.

'My old ma used to tell us that if you don't work you can expect to starve. No one tells kids that these days, and they grows up expecting everythin' for nothin'.'

Mrs Pringle joined in at this juncture.

'I blame the parents. Our Minnie's kids never goes to church, and they don't never learn the Ten Commandments. Why, we had to recite them to the vicar, didn't we, Bob?'

'That's right.'

'"Thou shalt not steal" was one of 'em. But Arthur Coggs don't remember that one. And he won't get punished, I'll lay.'

'Nobody don't,' agreed Bob Willet. 'Punishment's out! No wonder they grows up not knowing right from wrong.' He turned to me. 'You given 'em something to think about over that dropped gate?'

He blew out his moustache belligerently.

'Well, I haven't lashed about them with a horse-whip,' I said mildly, 'but I did give them a talking-to.'

Bob Willet and Mrs Pringle exchanged disgusted glances, and I thought it discreet to take my leave.

In Fairacre, as elsewhere, the older generation takes a poor view of those growing up, and I expect it was ever thus.

It was the loveliest May I could remember. My spirits were high, as I looked forward, with increasing excitement, to the end of term and my retirement.

I had no fears now about my health. In fact, I occasionally wondered if I had been over-anxious and given in my notice before time, but these doubts soon passed, and I revelled in the future before me.

The summer flowers began to adorn the classroom window-sills and my desk. Everything was early this year. The may buds were bursting on the hawthorn. Dandelions glowed on the grass verges, and the cottage gardens were gay with wall flowers, early pinks and irises.

Beside the massive brass inkstand, on my desk, a relic of a Victorian headmaster, stood an earthenware honey pot of equally ancient vintage, bearing a nosegay of clove pinks that scented the classroom with their spicy perfume.

One evening during this halcyon time of early summer, I had an unexpected visit from James, Amy's husband.

'I've been to see the Cottons,' he began, coming straight to the point. 'Have you been worrying about them?'

I had to admit that I had been a little perplexed about their finances but Bob Willet had heard that there was money owing on a Caxley clothing club.

'Well, I'm thankful to say we seem to have come to the bottom of things.'

It appeared that this was Mr Cotton's second marriage. His first wife had left him and had married again. By this first marriage they had had one daughter, now in her early twenties. She was a nurse at a large hospital in the north, and it was she who had caused the money problems.

'He's a very devoted father,' said James. 'We knew all about his matrimonial background when the Trust appointed him and the present Mrs Cotton to this post. The girl then was just about self-supporting, but she got into the clutches of an unscrupulous fellow who wheedled her savings from her, and then began to exert really menacing pressure. She turned to her father, who tried to extricate her from her troubles. He should have gone straight to the police, of course, but he was reluctant to get the daughter involved in court proceedings.'

'How did you find out?'

'I asked him what the trouble was. He seemed relieved to have someone to talk to. He's had a pretty awful time worrying about the present family, and letting the Trust down, and so on. Why he didn't tell us, I can't think. We'd have supported him and the girl. He's a jolly good father – one of our best.'

I marvelled, yet again, at James's ability to communicate with all sorts and conditions of men. It was not just his obvious charm and good looks. They were the outward expression of a true understanding of the other fellow's point of view, ready sympathy and a clear mind to sum up the problem and its handling.

'So how is the girl coping?'

'She's just become engaged to a young chap with his head screwed on. He's put the matter in the hands of the police, and luckily he is in a steady job, and they propose to marry this summer.'

'So it's a happy ending?'

'It looks like it. Mrs Cotton gave me a lovely kiss at the end of our little pow-wow.'

'I bet she did! Have a drink?'

'No. I'm driving; and I expect Amy has the grub waiting.'

I walked with him to the car. A blackbird was singing its heart out on a lilac bush.

'You've relieved my mind about the Cotton family,' I told him.

'That was the idea. Can't have your last few weeks at Fairacre clouded in any way.'

He gave me a farewell kiss which I found as satisfactory I imagine, as Mrs Cotton had, and off he went.

A day or two later, I encountered our vicar as I was coming back from Fairacre Post Office.

'What weather!' he enthused waving a hand and encompassing in the gesture the cottage gardens near at hand, the rooks wheeling round the church spire, and the hazy downs beyond.

'I know. Aren't we lucky?'

'I've just been to see Henry,' he told me. 'Have you seen him lately?'

'No. How is he?'

'Rather lonely, of course. I'm surprised he hasn't been to see you. Deirdre's away, you know.'

I said that I had heard.

Gerald Partridge began to look troubled, and stopped to flick non-existent dust from his shirt-front. I knew the signs. Our vicar was preparing to face a difficult few minutes.

'I'm just a little worried about him. He obviously misses his dear wife, and I should so like to see him settled happily.'

'We all should.'

He looked relieved.

'I know it is a long time ago,' he continued, 'soon after you came to Fairacre, but I know that we all hoped – wrongly, as it turned out – that you and Henry —' He faltered to a stop.

'I well remember it,' I told him, not wishing to be reminded of an embarrassing interlude.

'Of course, Henry was married already, but we did not know that,' he continued hastily. 'Now, of course, the poor fellow is permanently bereaved, and I must say I grieve for him.'

He began to move on again, and we approached the school gate. The playground was empty, and the hands of the church clock stood at four fifteen. The sun had moved round and was now streaming down on my car. It was going to be a hot drive home.

'I don't think I should worry too much about Henry,' I said. 'He has lots of good friends in Fairacre. Both of us, for instance.'

'That's true.'

The vicar began to look happier.

'And I'm sure he will find someone to look after him before long, and be happy again.'

'I do hope so. Of course, Deirdre is coming back soon, and they do seem —'

'Exactly,' I said firmly, and made for the car.

The vacancy caused by my impending departure had been advertised in the usual educational journals, and I remembered how I had applied so long ago. Then, of course, one of the greatest attractions for me had been the school house, providing handy accommodation so close to my duties. Now that the Umbleditches lived in my old home the new head teacher would have to look elsewhere for a house.

It should not be difficult to find somewhere, perhaps in Caxley itself, if not nearer at hand in one of the downland villages, for no doubt the new teacher would have a car.

I had not had one for some years after my appointment, and had not missed having private transport, for the buses then had been more frequent, and in any case, I trundled around on my bicycle then in those comparatively traffic-free country lanes. Now my successor could afford to live anywhere within a comfortable ten-, or even twenty-mile, radius of Fairacre school and still be in good time for morning assembly.

There had evidently been a number of applicants for the post, and towards the end of May they had been whittled down to four on the short list, two men and two women.

They were being called up for interview by the governors, and the meeting was to take place at the vicarage. I could visualise the scene, for I had often been invited to sit with the governors when a new assistant was being interviewed. On the present occasion, I should not attend.

The interviews were always held in the vicarage dining-room, an impressive Georgian room with a beautiful mahogany table. Gerald Partridge, as chairman of the governors, sat at the head, and there was ample room at each side for the applicants' papers, the governors' gloves, pens, diaries and other personal impedimenta, whilst the applicant's chair was placed in solitary state, at the far end, facing the chairman.

One of the most prominent features of the vicar's dining-room is a portrait of one of Gerald Partridge's ancestors. The old gentleman is holding a letter which our vicar is convinced was written by Charles II, rendering thanks to his forebear for services rendered to his king, when he was in exile, before the restoration of the monarchy.

The vicar is inordinately proud of this portrait, but I always found it rather depressing for the subject of the painting appears very cross, and no one could say that he was good looking. His descendant is certainly much more pleasant to behold.

As is customary, the four applicants had been invited to inspect the school before their interviews, and so I acted as hostess and general usher at this time.

I liked all four, and knew that I should be happy at the thought of any one of them taking my place next September. It would be interesting to see if a man was appointed, for in the past Fairacre had several headmasters over the years.

In those days, when the children stayed at the same school until they were fourteen, the bigger boys were often in need of fairly firm discipline as the great world loomed nearer. But since Fairacre school had been a junior primary school, for children from five to eleven years of age, for some years now, it had been usual to appoint a woman.

Which would it be this time, I wondered? And who, looking to the future, would follow George Annett at the larger school at Beech Green? There, I guessed, a headmaster would be appointed when George stood down, but for us, in Fairacre, it was anybody's guess.

The vicar had been kind enough to tell me the arrangements for the aftermath of the interviews. It had been decided to leave plenty of time for discussion by the governors after the interviews, and the applicants were each to be telephoned and given the decision during that evening.

'So much depends on getting the right person,' the vicar assured me. 'The applicants can make their way home, and know that they'll hear within a few hours, without having to sit all together while we come to a decision just after the meeting. I have always felt, too, that it is quite an ordeal for the lucky one to have to face his disappointed companions so soon after a trying time.'

'An ordeal for the others too,' I pointed out. 'I think this idea is perfect, and they can pour themselves a congratulatory – or commiserating – noggin, in the privacy of their own homes.'

'Just as we thought,' said the vicar, beaming.

I thought a good deal about my successor as I pottered about that evening. The head teacher of a village school holds an important place in the village hierarchy, as I knew to my cost.

I remembered Dolly Clare's accounts of the head teachers she had encountered during her lifetime.

She had started her school life in Caxley, but at the age of six the family had moved to Beech Green, and she had been entered on the register there a day or two after their arrival.

As a shy child, she had found the change upsetting. Luckily, the first person she came across at Beech Green school was Emily Davis, whose desk she shared on that first terrifying morning, and whose friendship started then and continued all their lives. In fact, as two old ladies, they had shared the cottage which was now my home, until Emily Davis had died tranquilly one night in the room which was now my spare bedroom.

The girls' first headmaster had been an energetic disciplinarian called Mr Finch, but on his retirement a new young man called Evan Waterman had taken his place.

Changes began immediately. He was a devout young man, inclining to such High Church practices as genuflection and much crossing of the breast, which alone alarmed his neighbours. He was also good-looking in a girlish way, and this too was cause for comment among the men.

The women were more tolerant, and the free-and-easy methods of teaching which had replaced Mr Finch's stern régime did not worry them unduly to begin with.

But later, it was apparent that such modern methods were too soon for most of the boys, and downright disobedience and mockery began to grow, until poor Evan Waterman was requested to find a post elsewhere.

Before his departure, Francis Clare, Dolly's thatcher father, had seen to it that Dolly was transferred to Fairacre school. Her dear friend Emily was also going there, and the two girls found themselves under the boisterous charge of Mr Wardle and his wife. Both demanded work of a high standard, but gave praise and encouragement under which their little school thrived.

It was from such accounts, as well as the reports in the ancient school log books, that one realised how much influence those earlier teachers had on their pupils, and for that matter, on the lives of all who dwelt with them in the villages.

I could only hope that I would be remembered with some affection, and that my successor would be as happy as I had been in charge of the school at Fairacre.

CHAPTER 13

Junketings

As an old hand at secret fundraising, I soon became conscious of the chink of coins being put into a screwtop honey jar in Mrs Richards' room.

I had seen this receptacle one morning when I had called to consult her about a letter from a parent, and it had been whisked so hastily into her desk drawer that I guessed that a leaving present for me was in the offing.

The vicar had broached the subject some weeks before and I had begged him not to present me with anything, unless perhaps a bunch of flowers, preferably from the village gardens.

But this, of course, fell on stony ground, and I could see that I was bound to receive something much more prestigious.

There was nothing for it but to submit with good grace, although I regretted this collecting of money when there was so much hardship in the village. Fairacre had suffered, along with the rest of the country, from the economic depression, for many of the fathers and mothers worked in Caxley at some of the new industries which had sprung up during the past twenty years. Quite a number had lost their jobs as the firms succumbed to bad times, and it worried me to think of money being spent on me at such a time.

However, I was realistic enough to know that I should

receive a leaving present, and I intended to accept it in the great-hearted spirit in which, I knew, it would be given.

The summer term had always been punctuated with such time-honoured events as Sports' Day, the Fête, and the Sunday school and choir outing. The last always took place on the first Saturday in July.

Before my time, as I had learnt from the vicar, and from the school log books, local schools closed for a fortnight for a fruit-picking holiday towards the end of June. At the end of that time when the families had usually earned some welcome extra money, a charabanc was hired and a day was spent by the sea.

In those days, this annual excursion to the sea was probably the only one and a great occasion it was.

Nowadays, when most families owned a car, or possibly two, the same excitement was not engendered by a day-trip to the seaside, but the first Saturday in July was still set aside for the outing and continued to be a highlight of the summer season. It would be my last in my capacity as head teacher, although no doubt I should be invited when I retired, just as Dolly Clare had been.

I contemplated my future with enormous pleasure. As far as one could tell, I should have the best of two worlds. I should be living in the same place, close to friends and neighbours with all that that implied. But I should also be free of constricting limits, such as the hours spent in school, and the necessity to prepare lessons or deal with official correspondence.

What was even more pleasurable now was the fact that my health seemed to have improved enormously since my decision to retire. Maybe the summer sunshine had something to do with it. Maybe the slackening of my duties had helped. Maybe the doctor's tablets and my early nights had something to do with this welcome feeling of good health.

Whatever the cause, I relished it after my alarms of the
winter. It had certainly sobered me, and made me realize
that robust health should never be taken for granted, but
simply as a bonus.

It was clear that June was going to be as glorious as May,
at least for the first few days.

Bob Willet, in his shirt sleeves at eight thirty in the
morning, bore witness to the warmth of the day to come.

'That cousin of Mr Mawne's is back,' he volunteered.

'*Mrs* Mawne,' I corrected him.

He looked startled. 'She ain't that already, is she?'

'Who d'you mean?'

'That Deirdre. Never did get her surname. She ain't
married him? You said "Mrs Mawne". That's quick work!'

I knew that this mistaken statement would be round the
village in a flash if I did not put it straight at once. This I
proceeded to do.

'I only meant that Deirdre is cousin to the late *Mrs*
Mawne and not *Henry* Mawne. And as far as I know, they
have no plans to marry.'

'Well, he looks ripe for it to my way of thinking.'

'I expect he's a little lonely.'

'And whose fault's that?' enquired Mr Willet, making
off before I could think of a reply.

The annual fête took place in the vicar's garden, as usual,
and despite ominous clouds at breakfast time, the weather
remained dry and firm.

The event was to be opened by someone known as a
'television personality', and expectations ran high.

'I've got his autograph,' boasted Ernest on the Friday
afternoon. 'I cut it out of the paper.'

'That's not a real autograph,' said Patrick. 'That's only

printed. You has to have the actual bit of paper what his hand rested on.'

He looked at me for support.

'Well, strictly speaking —' I began diplomatically, but was interrupted by the vicar appearing in a state of agitation.

'I fear that we are in for a disappointment. Our fête-opener is indisposed. I wonder who would step in at such short notice?'

'Couldn't you do it?'

He looked dismayed. 'I could, I suppose, but what a come-down for everyone.'

I thought otherwise, but said nothing.

'Do you think,' he said looking brighter, 'that our dear friend Basil Bradley would step in?'

Basil Bradley is a local novelist who writes historical novels with heroines in muslin frocks and ringlets, and heroes who fight duels on their behalf. The books sell in vast numbers, and everyone relishes a nice hour or two of escapism. Basil himself is modest and cheerful, and we are all very proud of him.

'If he's free I'm sure he'd come to the rescue,' I said.

He certainly did. The fête was duly opened with a short speech and many compliments to those who had helped to get it ready for general pleasure and the support of the Church Roof Fund, and we all set forth to enjoy ourselves.

The cake stall, as usual, was the first to be besieged and as Mrs Pringle was in charge this year there were very few goodies hidden behind the stall for favoured customers.

'Fair's fair!' she boomed, 'and those who comes first gets first pick. But it's all to be above board this year. *No* favourites!'

This stern dictum was surprisingly welcomed by her customers, and I wondered if the more easy-going earlier stall-holders would emulate her strict example in the years ahead.

I returned exhausted, and viewed my collection of articles bought, or won, at the kitchen table. I could eat the gingerbread, the lettuce and the eggs, but what about that rag doll and the highly scented bath salts, not to mention the Cyprus sherry and the pickled onions in a somewhat cloudy and dubious liquid?

'Give them to the next bazaar, of course,' I said aloud.

And Tibby gave an approving mew.

A day or two later Henry Mawne arrived at the school with a pile of bird magazines for our delectation.

'You weren't at the fête,' I said accusingly. 'You *never* miss the fête. What happened?'

He looked a little confused. 'I had to go to Heathrow to meet Deirdre. She's back for a short while.'

'Oh good! You'll have company.'

'Yes. You could say that, but I'm really giving her a hand over selling her place in Ireland.'

He sounded surprisingly business-like and important, and it dawned on me that usually his former wife had taken the decisions, which was probably one of the reasons why he missed her so much. Not that Henry lacked business sense. He has been in charge of the church funds for years, and the vicar relies on him for anything involving figures.

This was one of the reasons that Henry's absence from the fête perturbed me. Usually, the final figures are given to the parish an hour or so after the event has finished. Luckily, on this occasion, Mr Lamb from the Post Office had stepped into the breach.

Of course, I was intrigued to hear about Deirdre, and asked if she had found a cottage in our area. Or had she changed her plans?

'Well, no,' said Henry, looking a trifle hunted. 'She still hopes to find something. In fact, we looked at five or six before she went back to Ireland, but there was nothing that appealed to her.'

I recalled Bob Willet's words about Deirdre hoping to settle in with Henry himself, but naturally did not mention this.

'I hear you are going to the Oxford concert next week with John Jenkins,' he said. Was this carrying the attack into my own camp?

I said that I was.

'I wanted to ask you myself when the first notices went out, but my plans were so unsettled with Deirdre coming and going that I'm afraid I've missed the chance.'

At that moment I caught sight of John Todd about to stuff some sort of foliage – no doubt filched from the nature table – down the back of Joseph Coggs' shirt, and rushed to the rescue.

When I returned Henry was on his way out, waving a hand in farewell, and I was left to speculate.

What were his real feelings towards Deirdre? Was he becoming fonder of her, more protective, happier in her company? Or was she still the nuisance he seemed to find her earlier? And did she really want a house of her own, or were these delaying tactics until she had Henry – and his home – where she wanted?

And what about Henry's attitude to me? I felt somehow that it was changing. There was something a little malicious in the way he had mentioned John's invitation to the concert, and a hint of relief that he was out of the whole affair.

This, of course, was fine by me. I was obviously going to have more attention from my new friend than I really wanted, and it would be a relief to have dear old Henry engaged elsewhere.

I do my best to simplify life, but heaven alone knows it is uphill work sometimes.

On Saturday morning I went to Caxley to buy a new frock, or perhaps just a new blouse, to honour the concert with John.

I bumped into Amy, much to my delight, and we hastened to take coffee together. Naturally, she was very approving of my desire to improve my appearance and agog to hear about John.

'Now, don't throw away the chance of a happy future,' she began.

'I'm not. I'm looking forward to a wonderfully peaceful, *single* retirement.'

'Yes, yes, I know,' she said impatiently, 'but do think about this nice man. How disappointed he'll be if he is turned down. Why, he may even move elsewhere if he's badly hurt.'

'No chance of that,' I said, and rather rashly told her about his proposal.

Her surprise at this disclosure I found a trifle wounding. After all, why shouldn't I receive a proposal?

On the other hand, her frank dismay at my dismissal cheered me considerably.

'And you think he will ask you again? How can you be sure?'

'Well, he said he would. And I'm sure he's a man of his word.'

'Oh good,' she replied, sounding much relieved, and we went on to talk of James, and his skill at sorting out the Cottons' problems, and whether the enormous price I had just paid for a perfectly simply silk blouse was justified.

'Of course it is,' said Amy. 'Why, it may affect your whole future.'

'Amy,' I said, 'you are the most romantic woman I have ever met!'

'I wish I could say the same of you,' she retorted, as we parted.

The halcyon weather which we had enjoyed changed abruptly with a spectacular thunderstorm one June night.

The bedroom windows streamed with rain, and flashes of lightning lit up the countryside. The thunder shook the cottage, and Tibby scratched at my bedroom door, was admitted and dived for cover under the eiderdown.

Sleep was impossible, and it was almost four o'clock before the storm abated. I suppose I must have had a few hours' sleep, but when the alarm clock went off at seven I could have done with more.

But everything smelled wonderful after the rain. The clove pinks in the border gave out their spicy smell and the madonna lilies above them added to the morning's perfume.

The lane from Beech Green to Fairacre was still damp from the night's downpour, and steam was rising as the sun's strength grew. Small birds were busy foraging for insects which had ventured forth into the morning dampness, and larks were already up and away soaring into the blue above.

It was going to be a wonderful morning, but the weather man had warned us not to expect it to last, and sure enough, by mid-morning the clouds rolled in from the west, and by dinner time the rain was falling again.

'You're off to Oxford tonight, aren't you?' said Mrs Richards, as we dealt out school dinners.

I said that I was, and wondered yet again how she had acquired the news. Not from me, so presumably my date with John Jenkins was common knowledge. This did not surprise me after so many years of village life, but just *how* the rumours get about continues to flummox me.

I was home before four thirty in time to make myself a cup of tea before arraying myself in my new finery. John was to call for me at six and we were having a meal before the concert began.

I had invited him to eat at my house before we set off, but he was so quick to suggest a meal out that I was prompted to wonder if he did not like my cooking. However, it meant that I need not bother, and that was a welcome relief.

I think Amy would have been proud of my appearance, for the vastly expensive blouse was splendid, and went well with the older parts of the ensemble. Apart from the fact that I looked decidedly heavy-eyed from lack of sleep the previous night, I decided I was passable, even by Amy's standards.

The rain grew heavier as we set off, but we were both in good spirits as we neared Oxford. John had booked a table at an Italian restaurant near the concert hall, and we studied the menu. John predictably settled for a steak, but I ordered a delicious chicken breast stuffed with asparagus and ham.

As we waited for our food to arrive John said, 'Would you like today's proposal now, or as we go home?'

'Oh John! Must we have one at all?'

'Definitely. I'm working on the principle of water dripping on a stone. I think your heart is pretty flinty.'

'I deny it strongly. I take in stray cats and wounded birds, and always put spiders out of the window instead of squashing them.'

'But what about love-lorn middle-aged men?'

'I'm extremely kind to them and go to concerts with them.'

'So shall it be now or later?'

'Let's have it now.'

'"And get it over", I expect you to say! So, here goes. Is there any change in that stony heart?'

I smiled at him. Give him his due, he was a trier.

'Not really, John. I shouldn't bother any more if I were you.'

He shook his head but he was smiling too, as the waiter arrived with our food.

I thoroughly enjoyed our meal, the concert and John's company throughout the evening.

I liked him even more when he declined my invitation to have a drink when he dropped me at my door, gave me a kindly kiss, and drove off in good spirits.

A nice man, but not for me.

The vicar and his wife had been away for a few days, but on his return he called at the school to tell me of the governors' decision.

They had appointed one of the women, Miss Jane Summers, and I knew at once that the children, and their parents, would wholeheartedly approve.

If I had favoured any one of the four candidates it would have been this person. She was large and jolly, in her thirties, and looked as though she had enough energy and humour to cope with all the problems which would confront her.

Even Mrs Pringle grudgingly admitted that 'she looked a *motherly* sort', who would be a comfortable figure for the new babies to confront on their first school day.

'But how she'll get on with them little monsters of boys in your room,' she said gloomily, 'the Lord alone knows. They could do with the strap now and again. The state of my lobby floors this week is enough to break your heart.'

I said, not quite truthfully, that I felt sure that Miss Summers would be as anxious about the lobby floors as she was herself.

'Well, that'll make a nice change,' said the old harridan. 'When have *you* worried youself about them, I'd like to know!'

She made her way out with no hint of a limp. Any such little triumph does her bad leg a world of good.

Mr Willet was less censorious, but cautious in his approach to a new set of circumstances.

'I don't like changes, as well you know, and I daresay this new lady will do her best, and no doubt we'll all shake down together in good time. But I tell you straight, Miss

Read, you've been a treat to work for, and me and Alice'll be real sorry to see you go. You've been a proper headmistress, and you'll be missed.'

I only wished that Mrs Pringle had been present to hear such compliments, but she, of course, was in the lobby grieving over the floor.

Naturally, the news of the appointment went through the village with the speed of a bush fire, and I received a great many comments.

Mr Lamb said that he was sure the new head would be welcomed but, he added gallantly, no one could possibly take my place. He wished though that a man had been appointed, for some of those boys could do with a clip now and again, and women were a bit soft that way.

Alice Willet said she wished I'd change my mind and stay on. Mr Roberts, the farmer, said he liked the look of the new woman. He always thought fat women were better tempered. Nothing personal, mind you, and if you were a bit skinny it couldn't be helped, but give him a plump woman every time.

The two newcomers, Mrs Bennett and Mrs Cotton, were inclined to be tearful, which I found surprising. But they pointed out that they had only just got used to me, and my school ways, and there I was *gone*!

Eve and Horace Umbleditch said it was a pity their boy would not have the inestimable privilege of starting his school career under my guidance, and that Jane Summers, no matter how worthy and clever, could never be a patch on me. Nevertheless, they agreed that I was Doing the Right Thing and Horace was already counting the years to his own retirement.

It was all very flattering, and I was duly grateful for these unsolicited tributes. But why, I wondered, did it need my retirement to prompt these kindly compliments?

In future, I told myself, I should make a point of expressing my admiration and respect for any deserving person who crossed my path and was still hale enough to relish my remarks.

The vicar called to remind the children about the outing on the following Saturday, and then drew me aside in a conspirational manner.

'I have been asked to request you to make a list of things you would like as your leaving present, so that the committee could choose something that you really want.'

'Oh, but please, you know that I really don't —' I began, but was cut short.

'Just jot down a few ideas. The whole village wants to contribute, and we already have a vast sum, so let us know what you would like.'

I stammered my gratitude to his retreating back, and sat down feeling stunned.

What was 'a vast sum'?

Knowing our vicar's complete lack of financial understanding I thought it might be anything from five pounds to five hundred. And in any case one could hardly ask him what 'a vast sum' was.

Here was a problem. I really had no idea what I wanted. I knew that I needed some new nail scissors, but it did not seem quite the thing to put on the list.

I decided to shelve the problem until I got home, and as soon as I had refreshed myself with tea I set to work.

But before I began, Amy arrived with a bunch of roses from her garden, and was greeted with even more delight than usual.

'They're gorgeous,' I cried, taking them from her. 'I'll put them in a vase.'

'They could really do with a rose bowl,' said Amy,

looking round hopefully. 'I'll do them for you. I don't care for your grip-and-drop-in arrangements.'

I refused to take umbrage.

'You shall have a choice of vases,' I told her. 'I've never had a rose bowl.'

As she arranged them in two vases, I told her about my problem. She immediately began to organize things, much to my relief.

'How much is this "vast sum"?'

'That's the snag. I've no idea, and I don't want them to spend a lot on me. They know that, but they won't listen.'

'Well, we shall just have to make a list with a good range of price. Anything in the kitchen line you'd like?'

'The back-door mat is pretty shabby.'

'That's not suitable for the list,' said Amy in a brisk manner. 'What about a new gadget? Have you got a food-mixer?'

'I don't want a food-mixer. I should have to wash it up, and I'd be bound to lose all the twiddly bits.'

'A microwave? A steam iron? A coffee-maker?'

'Ah! D'you mean like yours? With a lid that pushes down over the grounds?'

'Yes. A cafetière.'

'I'd like that.'

'Well, at least we've made a start,' said Amy, writing busily.

'Now,' she went on, fixing me with a sharp eye, 'we'll take it room by room. Anything needed in the dining-room?'

After some heavy thought I decided that a sauce boat and new table mats could go down.

'Sitting-room?' said Amy briskly. 'I should think you might ask for a silver rose bowl.'

'I'd never use it. Besides I'd have to polish it. Perhaps another table lamp might be useful, or a clock.'

'You'd better be careful about a clock,' advised Amy, 'or you'll get landed with a black marble job in the form of a Greek temple like those that dominated our grandparents' mantelpieces.'

'I could stipulate a small brass carriage clock,' I suggested.

'Excellent,' approved Amy. 'Now for upstairs. What's wanted there?'

'I really need a new face flannel,' I said thoughtfully.

Amy threw down her pen in exasperation. 'You can't ask for a *face flannel*,' she protested.

'I know I can't. But you did ask me.'

She retrieved her pen.

'What about a hand-held shower?'

'Too messy. I'd sooner get in the tub.'

'Anything in the bedroom?'

'Oh, Amy, I can't be bothered any more! Let's have a turn in the garden.'

It was bliss out there, fresh and scented under a pale blue sky. We felt better at once.

'Tell you what,' said Amy, 'you could do with a nice plain teak garden seat, to replace that poor decrepit thing over there. Or a bird bath. Or even a nesting box or two.'

'The seat sounds rather expensive, but the others could go down.'

'Put the seat down too. This "vast sum" might well run to it.'

'Perhaps a small one,' I said weakening. 'A two-seater, say.'

Amy was looking round in a contemplative manner.

'Of course, if it really is "a vast sum" you could rethatch the cottage, or buy a new car. Haven't you any idea of how much this "vast sum" might be?'

I told her that the vicar's idea of a 'vast sum' could be anything around a hundred pounds.

'It's so difficult,' agreed Amy. 'You see, if James used that expression he would be talking about several millions.'

'Well, it won't be that, I'm thankful to say,' I told her. 'Let's go in and add those garden ideas to the list.'

We did that, refreshed ourselves with a glass of sherry, and I saw her on her way.

At least I had a list of sorts to offer the vicar, thanks to Amy's firm direction.

What should we do without our friends?

CHAPTER 14

The Outing

The day of the outing dawned still and bright, and we gathered at eight thirty sharp, as directed by the vicar, outside the Post Office at Fairacre.

The bus was already there and we scrambled aboard. Joseph Coggs elected to sit by me, and was kind enough to offer me an unwrapped mint humbug, rather fluffy from his pocket, but I explained that it was a little too early in the day for me to eat sweets, and he nodded cheerfully and ate it himself.

To my surprise, I saw that Henry and Deirdre were approaching and were soon settled across the gangway. Henry was looking very relaxed in a striped blazer, and Deirdre, true to form, had arrived with a gauzy blue scarf round her head, but this was removed when they had settled in their seats.

Henry, of course, as the vicar's right-hand man, had sometimes accompanied us on the annual outing, but I had not expected to see him this time as I knew that Deirdre would be at his house.

We exchanged chit-chat as we bowled along, and I thought that Deirdre seemed rather more animated than usual. Perhaps Henry's presence was stimulating.

I remembered the last time Henry, Deirdre and I had taken a bus trip together to the falconry, and how embarrassing I had found Henry's attentions to me, and his marked coolness towards his guest. It was a relief to have him less tiresome, but I was glad too to have Joseph Coggs ensconced at my side.

How well I remembered an earlier trip to the seaside resort of Barrisford, for which we were bound again this morning. As usual, after an outing, I had suggested to the children, during the following week, that they might draw a picture of something that they had enjoyed during that day.

Joseph had come up with the picture of a small man who, he insisted, was the Old Man of the Sea and had a palace on the sea bed beyond the end of Barrisford pier. He had stuck to his story adamantly, although we found out later that he had encountered one of the midget acrobats who were appearing that week in an end-of-pier show.

As far as I knew, Joseph still believed the story which had been told him, and even now, I surmised, he might be hoping to encounter him again.

Barrisford remained the most popular choice for our annual outing. Sometimes we had changed our destination and had visited Longleat and its animals, Bournemouth with its variety of entertainment and other renowned resorts on the south coast. But somehow we always returned to Barrisford, to its shining sands, its quiet respectability, and above all, to tea at Bunce's, the famous restaurant on the esplanade where Mr Edward Bunce himself waited upon us with never-failing courtesy.

Barrisford, we all agreed, was the *real* place to go for an outing.

Most of the party dispersed to the sands, but Deirdre made a point of joining me and suggested that we took ourselves

to Bunce's for a refreshing cup of coffee. Henry waxed enthusiastic.

When we were settled at a table overlooking the bay, I enquired how the house-hunting was getting on.

'We looked at two yesterday,' said Henry. 'Quite possible, I thought.'

'I didn't,' said Deirdre. 'They were poky.'

'Most cottages are,' I agreed, 'but that has its advantages. Less to heat, less to clean, and usually pretty snug.'

'One was near Springbourne,' went on Henry, ignoring his companion's dislike of the topic, 'on the hill there. Lovely views.'

'Not a house in sight,' said Deirdre with disgust. 'One would go melancholy mad.'

The coffee arrived at this moment and the subject of

houses was dropped until a little later when Deirdre had departed to the ladies' room and Henry and I were alone.

'I fear that Deirdre wants somewhere with bigger rooms. She's got used to living in my house, you know, and I think it has influenced her choice overduly.'

I thought of Henry's magnificent rooms in part of the Queen Anne house which had been old Miss Parr's when I first went to Fairacre. It would be hard to find such elegance in the small houses Deirdre was inspecting.

Henry sighed, and put his hand on mine by the coffee pot.

'If only things had been different,' he said.

I looked at him squarely. 'But they aren't, Henry, and never have been. At least on my side.'

'I had hoped,' he began, 'when I first came —'

'Henry, I don't care to think about that time. You meant nothing to me, except in a friendly way, and you know what a bundle of trouble village gossip put us to.'

He removed his hand, and stood up to welcome back Deirdre who had removed the gauzy scarf and looked, to my eyes at least, very attractive.

'Now I shall see you two settled,' said Henry, 'and then I'm off for a swim. Nothing like salt water!'

I was about to say, 'Probably laced with sewage', but felt it was kinder to remain silent. Henry had had quite enough chastening for one day, I decided.

Deirdre and I sat in the shelter of a rock and watched our fellow villagers disporting themselves on land and sea.

Henry was being splashed vigorously by three or four of my schoolchildren, but was giving as much as he was getting, amidst shrieks of delight.

'I'm very fond of Henry,' remarked Deirdre languidly. 'What do you think of him?'

'He's always been a good friend. Not only to me. Everyone in the village likes him.'

Deirdre gazed out to sea. Henry's head was now bobbing in the foreground.

'He's very fond of you. My cousin, you know, never really appreciated Henry. In fact, she stayed with me in Ireland for nearly two years, she was so fed up with him.'

I remained silent. I well remembered Henry's time alone when Fairacre supposed that he was a bachelor or widower, and well qualified to marry a single school teacher.

'She was horribly bossy,' said Deirdre. 'Henry never had a say in anything. He needed *kindness*, and I think that's why he was attracted to you.'

I was startled into speech. I had not thought of *kindness* as one of my more obvious virtues.

'I can assure you that I had no idea that Henry was attracted to me at that time. I must admit there was some village gossip, but one ignores that.'

'Well, it was largely that which brought his wife back to him. She may not have wanted him herself, but she did not intend to part with him. I was quite relieved to see her go.'

She looked out to sea again. Henry seemed to have vanished.

'Poor Henry,' she sighed. 'He has had a sad life. I think it is time he was shown some affection and consideration, don't you?'

'We can all do with that,' I assured her.

She turned her eyes from the sea, and looked steadily at me. 'When you retire, will you be lonely?'

'Not for a moment,' I said, knowing full well what prompted this solicitude on my behalf.

'I'm so glad we had this little talk,' she said, rising and dusting sand from her skirt. 'It makes things much easier for me.'

'Good luck with your house-hunting, and all your other projects,' I said, as we set off for a companionable saunter along the famous sands.

Tea at Bunce's was the highlight of the afternoon, and at six thirty we were all aboard again, wind-blown and sun-burnt, bound for Fairacre.

I was dropped off in Beech Green, only a few yards from my home, and waved farewell to my fellow passengers, as the bus moved off.

Deirdre gave me a broad smile and, I could have sworn, a wink at the same time.

Mightily content, I turned for home.

On Monday morning, Mrs Pringle limped heavily towards me and I feared the worst.

'I've got that dratted Basil all next week,' she greeted me, 'and I wondered if he could come up here. Next term he starts at Beech Green, and welcome they are to him, and no mistake.'

'Is Minnie ill?'

'She's got a little job up at Springbourne Manor. Just for next week.'

I was surprised to hear it. Minnie is well known for her complete lack of common sense, and has no idea how to tackle housework. I asked what she was being called upon to do at such a well-run establishment.

'They're cleaning out the stables. Some talk of them being turned into houses, and they've got two great skips up there to throw all the rubbish in. She's helping to fill 'em up.'

It seemed the sort of thing she might manage, but I wondered how many objects, later needed, would be the victims of Minnie's activity.

'But isn't the work rather heavy for Minnie?'

Mrs Pringle's countenance became even more gloomy than usual.

'The fact is they need the money. Them kids eats like oxen.'

I began to fear that all this was a preliminary to asking me to supply work for Minnie.

I was right.

'I don't suppose you could give her a couple of hours, now and again?'

'Mrs Pringle,' I began bravely, 'you know as well as I do that Minnie is absolutely hopeless in the house.'

The old curmudgeon had the grace to look abashed at this straight speaking.

'I was thinking about your brights. If she was to come, say, once a month, when I was there of a Wednesday, I could keep an eye on her and see she got out the Brasso and not the stuff to clean the oven. She couldn't do much harm cleaning brass and copper. Particularly your things.'

I did not care for this slur on my property, but overlooked it in the face of this larger menace.

'We could try it, I suppose,' I said weakly, 'but not just yet.'

'Mrs Partridge is having her to scrub out the back kitchen, and the old dairy and wash house, on a Wednesday morning. She's to have her dinner there too.'

Not for the first time, I saw Mrs Partridge as a true Christian, and a worthy wife for our vicar. In the face of such nobility of character, I began to review my own skimpy offering of help.

'She can start after the end of term,' I told Mrs Pringle.

And knew that I should regret it.

A week or two later, the school Sports' Day took place, and everyone prayed for the same sort of halcyon weather which had blessed our trip to Barrisford.

Mr Roberts, the local farmer, always lets us use the field

next to our school for our Sports' Day. He removes his
house cow, who normally grazes there, and supplies stakes
and rope to fence off the course itself.

Mr Willet, a few of the bigger boys and I usually spend
an hour or so, on the evening before, getting the field
ready for competitors, parents and other visitors.

The main task is roping off the sports area, and stamping
down the largest of the molehills. The grass is tussocky in
places, and any professional runner would blench at the
hazards of racing on such terrain, but we are made of
sterner stuff in Fairacre and cope with these little difficulties
without complaint.

Sadly, the weather was far from perfect. A boisterous
wind blew hair and skirts, and even threatened to overturn
the blackboard on which Mrs Richards recorded the results.
Chairs and benches had been brought from the school and
village hall by Mr Roberts' tractor and trailer, and hardy
parents and friends of the school bravely sat by the dividing
rope, with the collars of their coats turned up against the
breeze.

But at least the rain held off, and the infants stole the
show with their sack race, seconded only by the parents'
race which was won by our newcomer to the village, Mrs
Bennett, amidst great enthusiasm.

It was half-past four when all was over. The chairs were
piled upon the waiting trailer, the blackboard and easel
manhandled back to their rightful place, and Mr Willet
remained surveying the stakes and rope with a mallet in his
hand.

Clouds were piling up in the west as children and
parents departed, and I urged Bob Willet to leave his
duties until tomorrow.

'Mr Roberts said as much,' I informed him. 'There's
nothing there to hinder anyone overnight.'

'Then I'll be getting home,' he said, and departed.

I went back to the empty schoolroom to collect a few more of the belongings which had accumulated there over the years and which I was gradually transferring to my home or, more often, to the school dustbin.

There was no one in the building. Mrs Pringle had finished her ministrations and gone. Mrs Richards was halfway to Caxley to prepare Wayne's evening meal. The only sound was the measured tick-tock of the great clock on the wall, and I sat at my desk relishing the silence.

How many head teachers had sat here before me during the long life of this little school? Had I wished, I could have reached down to the bottom drawer of the desk at which I now sat, and lifted out the three great log books which recorded all that had gone before.

The opening entry had been made in 1880 by the first headmistress. She had been helped by her sister who was in charge of the babies' class. Ever since its opening the school had been a two-teacher establishment, as it was today. Sometimes a headmaster ruled, sometimes a headmistress, and very soon yet another headmistress would follow in my footsteps and be, I sincerely hoped, as happy as I had been.

This modest and shabby little building must have seen remembered by thousands of country people over its long history. Soldiers in the Boer War, the Great War of 1914–18, and the war which overshadowed our own lifetime had come from this classroom, had heard the clock tick as I did now, and had memories, no doubt, in those far-off and perilous times of a small and peaceful place where the rooks wheeled about the church spire and the scent of honeysuckle wafted in from the vicarage garden hard by.

Many former pupils had died overseas, for there was a strong attraction from America and from New Zealand where several families had emigrated at the turn of the century. But many pupils lay close by their school, in the churchyard of St Patrick's, among their old friends. And on the walls of the nave and chancel were many lists, poignantly long for such a tiny village, of those who had perished in battle.

Very soon Jane Summers would be sitting here, heiress, as I had been, to this little kingdom which wielded unknown power to influence so many future lives.

It was a sobering, but strangely uplifting thought, to know that one was just a link in a long chain:

> *. . . a poor player,*
> *That struts and frets his hour upon the stage,*
> *And then is heard no more.*

St Patrick's clock began to strike six. I gathered up my belongings and went outside towards the car.

As I was locking the school door I suddenly remembered an occasion when I had returned towards the end of summer holiday, and had found the gossamer threads of a spider across the closed door jamb. It was at a time when we had feared that Fairacre school would have to close because of falling numbers, and I had had the chill feeling that soon the signs of neglect and desertion would engulf the little place.

Cobwebs, dead leaves, the musty smell of an abandoned building would be its lot, and I had been shaken with sudden sadness.

Now I locked up with a braver heart. Thanks to the Trust's efforts and the two new families in our midst, that cloud had been lifted from us, and Jane Summers, and her successors, could look forward to continuing the tradition of our little school.

CHAPTER 15

Farewell to Fairacre School

The last day of any term is usually greeted with unalloyed joy and relief, by pupils and teachers alike.

This was no exception when I splashed happily in the bath tub, but as I sat at the breakfast table, looking out into a pearly quiet garden, a little shiver of apprehension cooled the glow of anticipation.

I was not worried about the larger issues of my retirement. Any doubts about the wisdom of my move had been sorted out and I had come to terms with my future plans.

What worried me now was the immediate programme of the day. There would be some emotional hurdles to overcome, and I felt some dread about my ability to cope with them.

For a start, the vicar had insisted on coming to take morning assembly, when no doubt he would make reference to my departure. Should I be mentioned in the prayers? I could certainly do with some support from church quarters, and any other for that matter, but would the vicar discourse too enthusiastically on my merits, if any, and his hopes for my future?

And then there was the presentation to face in the afternoon. The secret of what form it would take had been well kept, and I had no idea of what was going to be given to me.

I knew that I must make a speech of thanks, and had already planned that it would be short, sincere and simple. The most awful fear was that I might break down and weep. I shuddered at the thought.

Mrs Richards, I felt sure, would shed a few tears, as she was easily moved, confessing that a brass band or flags waving 'set her off'. I had already determined to see that she was placed well out of range of my vision, in case I wept in sympathy.

Oh dear, I thought, as I cleared away the breakfast things, how I *hate* publicity! My heart sank at the thought of all those people – no matter how well known and kindly disposed – and I remembered the fuss my poor mother had to face, years earlier, when I was forced to go to a party.

It was useless to point out that my friends would be there, that people would not have invited me if they did not want my company. The stark fact remained that I should have to be properly dressed, be particularly polite and, worst of all, act as though I were really enjoying myself.

Well, I told myself, searching for the car keys, I coped then, and I supposed that I could cope today.

Time alone would tell.

Mrs Richards was in school when I arrived and looked a little tearful already, much to my alarm. She was leafing through *Hymns Ancient and Modern*.

'I'm trying to find something suitable,' she said. 'You know, something really memorable.'

'Well, keep off "Abide With Me," and "Lead Kindly Light", I beg of you. What about "Praise my Soul"?'

'But that seems so *heartless*, as though we're glad to see you go, which we aren't.'

She began to look even more woebegone.

'I've got a soft spot for "Ye Holy Angels Bright" and I don't think it's too difficult to play.'

She began to turn the pages.

'If you really want that, then you should have the choice this morning,' she said, more cheerfully, and I left her to strum a few chords whilst I unlocked my desk.

Mrs Pringle, when she arrived, was almost smiling. No doubt with relief at seeing me on duty for the last time, was my uncharitable thought, but I was soon enlightened.

'I had a notice from the office. Wages are going up. Not much, mind you, but every little helps.'

I gave her my congratulations.

'It's no more than it should be by rights. That office can have no idea of what's wanted, trying to keep this place decent. Why, the stoves alone are one woman's work, and those everlasting boots all over the lobby floors, day in and day out —'

She was forced to take breath.

'You know it's been appreciated,' I said, feeling that I could afford to be magnanimous on my last morning.

'It's all right for *some*,' continued Mrs Pringle. 'Come tomorrow they'll be free of all this. Plenty of time to take it easy while the drudgery goes on and on for others.'

'Time for the bell,' I said briskly, and Mrs Pringle limped painfully out of sight.

Mrs Richards and I exchanged meaningful glances as Ernest burst into the room to ring the school bell.

The vicar, I was relieved to see, was much as usual, rather absent-minded and vague, and certainly entirely free from embarrassing emotion.

He always came on the last day of term, but had he forgotten that it was my very last day at Fairacre school? I need not have worried.

In the final prayer he mentioned 'servants who had served for many years with grace and unfailing cheerfulness', which I presumed referred to my endeavours, in the kindest possible way, and also to 'the hope that such servants, and in particular our own dear school teacher, should enjoy the bounty of a long and happy retirement', which I silently endorsed.

'I shall see you again at two o'clock,' he said, as he departed, and I chided myself for thinking that he would forget any of his duties. I should have known better after all these years.

There was a general air of excitement about the classroom that morning, and I knew that the secret they had so faithfully kept was contributing to it.

The atmosphere was not conducive to mental work, and in any case, most of the exercise books and text books were already neatly packed away ready for Jane Summers' over-seeing next term. We confined ourselves, in the usual end-of-term way, to paper games such as the old favourites, 'How many words can you make from CONSTANTINOPLE?', and 'How many boys' and girls' names can you think of beginning with S?'

More worldly children need videos and computers, but in Fairacre we still enjoy pencils and paper, I am glad to say.

I noticed that the lobby was unusually fragrant when I saw the children out at playtime. A chair, draped with a tea towel, screened what I guessed was a mammoth bunch of flowers, and I could smell lilies, roses, pinks, honeysuckle, a mixture of delicious scents. I diverted my eyes from the screen as I saw the children through the door, and was equally virtuous when I returned for my morning coffee.

The dinner lady brought us shepherd's pie with young carrots and calabrese, with pink blancmange for our pudding. The latter is a great favourite with the children as it is decorated with blobs of white stuff which the children call cream, but which I find unidentifiable.

She also presented me with a box of chocolates, kissed me warmly and said she would miss me. I began to feel dangerously tearful, but responded with equal warmth.

How nice to think that I should be missed!

By two o'clock there was a throng in the school playground, and luckily the sun shone and the boisterous downland wind was not in evidence.

A few chairs had been put here and there for those in need, but I was relieved to see that most visitors would be expected to stand. At least it showed that the proceedings would be brief.

A large object, draped in one of Mr Roberts' tarpaulins, stood in a prominent position. It could be a refectory table or a chest of drawers, but I secretly hoped it might prove to be a garden seat, although I had been appalled at the price shown in a gardening catalogue I had looked at. This had been *after* I had given the list to the vicar, and I had had a few bad moments about it.

It was a very large alien object in our playground, but I did my best to ignore it.

St Patrick's church clock struck two o'clock, and a few moments later the vicar clapped his hands for silence, and the ceremony began.

During the vicar's opening address, I had time to study the visitors. Among them Mr Willet stood to one side, and I was touched to see that he was in his best blue serge suit. Mrs Pringle too, was formally dressed and wearing a navy blue straw hat with a duck's wing spread along its ample brim, a real go-to-meetings hat, and its presence today I counted as a great honour.

The younger mothers, of course, were hatless and pretty in their summer frocks. Half a dozen toddlers roamed about, and I thought, with a pang, that I should not be teaching them when their time came. It was little sharp pin-pricks such as this that periodically jerked me into reality.

Someone from the county education office then said some more kind things, and Mrs Bennett, representing the parents and very shy about it, added her tribute.

The moment had arrived for the vicar, helped by Bob Willet, to throw off the tarpaulin covering the mysterious object, and this they did with a great flourish, displaying a magnificent garden seat to the admiration of us all.

It was overwhelmingly generous, and I began to wonder if I should be able to get through my carefully rehearsed speech without breaking down.

I stood up, took a deep breath and began my speech. To my horror I found that my voice was shaky, and that I had a painful lump in my throat. At the same moment I caught sight of Mrs Richards' face, streaming with tears. I began to wonder if I should soon be in the same state.

At this dreadful moment, a large Labrador puppy rushed across the playground, much to the indignation and dismay of my audience.

The vicar nobly attempted to grab the animal, but it romped towards the crowd, delighted to find so many playmates.

Voices rose.

'That's the pub's!'

'Always loose, that dog!'

'Those new people at the Beetle and Wedge have no idea!'

'Catch his collar, Ernest!'

'It's too bad. Miss Read's last day too!'

The puppy bounded about, resisting all attempts at capture. The children were even more excited and vociferous than their elders, and increased the animal's antics.

At last Bob Willet grabbed its tail, and then its collar, and dragged it into the school lobby and shut the door.

By this time I had collected myself, blown my nose, and was beginning to feel amusement rather than trepidation. I was able to go on with my speech, despite a background of yelps, whines and howls from the lobby. I sat down to a storm of applause.

The vicar was full of apologies which he shouted in my ear against even more prolonged clapping, and the meeting ended in general surging of all present, as we went to inspect my lovely present, and to greet each other.

Mr Roberts produced a length of binder twine from his pocket.

'I always carry a bit about me,' was his comment, and he went to secure the puppy and return it to the pub.

'I'm coming straight back,' he told me, 'to take your seat over to your place in the pick-up. Don't you hurry yourself. Bob's giving me a hand, and he knows just where to put it in your garden.'

'One moment,' said the vicar, 'we want a photograph of Miss Read on the seat, with all the school around her. Mr Lamb has brought his camera with him.'

We settled ourselves on my new possession. I sat in the middle and there was room for two squashed children on each side.

Mrs Richards stood behind me. While Mr Lamb fiddled importantly with the camera, she leant over and said with some agitation, 'Little Betty was supposed to be giving you a bouquet, but we dare not go into the lobby because of the dog. Can we present it after this?'

'Of course. How kind you all are!'

'Ready?' shouted Mr Lamb.

We all smiled, and John Todd held up two fingers in what I hoped was the V sign, as the camera clicked.

'Just another for good luck,' said Mr Lamb, and I was able to tell John Todd to put his hands away before the next click.

The vicar, who had been apprised of the bouquet incident, now requested everyone to wait, and the youngest child in the school emerged from the lobby carrying a bunch of flowers nearly as big as herself.

There was renewed clapping. I made a second speech of thanks, and very slowly some of the crowd began to drift homeward.

I went to collect my things from indoors. Mrs Pringle was surveying the lobby floor with a doom-laden face.

'As if it ain't bad enough with *children*, let alone *dogs*.'

It was a fitting farewell, I thought, as I collected my belongings.

I was home before the garden seat arrived, and was just about to put on the kettle when Amy arrived.

'I thought you might be feeling a bit low,' she said. 'It must have been a daunting day for you.'

'To be honest,' I said, 'it really hasn't sunk in yet. Such a lot happened.' I told her about the speeches and the presents and the dog and the photographs, and we agreed that a cup of tea was absolutely essential after all that.

Amy went out to her car as I set the tray, and returned with a pot containing a rose bush.

'It's one of the "Peace" variety called something like "Hope" or "Happy Future", but I seem to have lost the label.'

'It's heavenly,' I said, 'and marks the occasion perfectly.'

Mr Roberts and Bob arrived as we were pouring out, but having deposited the seat where my shabby old one once stood, they refused to join us, saying that they were now off to Springbourne to help with the cricket sight screen which was in a poor way.

'I'm not saying "goodbye",' Mr Roberts said, pecking my cheek. 'You'll be turning up in Fairacre again like a bad penny, I'll bet.'

'And I'll see you tomorrow,' added Bob, eyeing Amy's present. 'I'll put that in proper. I can see it's a beauty. I'll bring young Joe Coggs with me to hold it steady.'

We waved them goodbye, and returned to our tea cups.

'By the way,' said Amy, 'I hope you'll keep the last week of September free.'

'What's happening?'

'James is off to Florence for a conference. He'll be closeted in meetings all the time, so I hope you'll keep me company and we'll go sightseeing.'

'Perfect. But only if we go Dutch.'

'We'll see about that nearer the time,' said Amy. 'But what about the immediate future? I don't want you moping about regretting your decision.'

'I promise you I shan't do that. I've got the Annetts to tea tomorrow, and I'm going to Rousham with John next week, to see the garden.'

'Oh, I'm so glad! Perhaps he'll propose again.'

'I've no doubt about it. It's a regular occurrence.'

'So there's hope for you yet,' exclaimed Amy, looking so excited that I had not the heart to disappoint her.

*

It was when I was in bed that night that I began to think.

How kind everybody had been, overwhelming me with gifts and compliments! It had been a wonderful day, and I should never forget it, the culmination of many years of teaching in a village school.

To many it would seem a dull life, virtually untouched by great national events, and simple to the point of being humdrum.

But I had been happy in it. The day-to-day activities in what Oliver Goldsmith called 'the vale of obscurity' suited me and would provide me with many memories as, I felt sure, it would provide a lifetime of memories for the hundreds of children who had shared Fairacre school with me.

I thought of all those teachers who had preceded me, and who had made their contribution to the school.

Lying there, in Dolly Clare's bedroom, I remembered with affection her particular contribution to those who knew her. She had set an example of serenity and gentleness, and above all of bravery in adversity.

Nevertheless, I had done my best. I had been happy, and had encouraged the children to find happiness in the downland about them.

Perhaps that would be my small contribution to the history of Fairacre, making children aware of the wonders about them.

I found it a fitting epitaph.

CHAPTER 16

Afterwards

It is exactly two months since my last school day, and I have had time to get used to retirement.

The children are back at school, and I see them in the playground at Beech Green school as I saunter, in a leisurely way, to my local shop. At Fairacre, no doubt, there is the same shouting, rushing about and general mayhem, but now I am spared that.

Jane Summers has been to tea, and I can see that we are going to be good friends. She is cheerful, sensible, fond of her little flock, and I think that Fairacre school is lucky to have her to guide its fortunes.

Two more children have been added to the roll, and it looks as if the school faces a steady future.

Mrs Pringle continues to visit me on Wednesday afternoons, occasionally threatening to give the place a 'good bottoming' as it now gets even dirtier than before, as I am in it so much. Minnie has been twice, and I have seen her aunt settle her firmly at the kitchen table with the correct cleaning materials and my pieces of copper and brass. So far, no real damage has been done, although she was about to attack my gold wristwatch with Brasso when I had foolishly left it on the windowsill.

I enjoyed my second visit to Rousham with John, and we have had several jaunts together elsewhere. So far I

have received seven proposals of marriage, and together
we have brought the art of offer-and-polite-decline to a
very high standard.

In a week or so I go to Florence with Amy and James,
and relish seeing that lovely city in September sunshine.
The thought of being on holiday, and permanent holiday
at that, will add spice to this adventure.

Bob Willet is a regular visitor, occasionally bringing
Joseph Coggs as his assistant. He told me last time that
Arthur Coggs has been given a spell of probation for his
recent offences. The Caxley magistrates had been much
impressed by the psychiatric report which found Arthur
'deeply disturbed'.

'And so am I,' stated Bob Willet grimly, 'when I know
Arthur's loose again.'

The two new families, housed by the Trust, are now
firmly settled into our village ways, and the younger
members will soon be among the pupils of Fairacre
school.

But the most exciting news is that Henry Mawne has
married Deirdre at a quiet ceremony in Ireland, and that
he will be bringing his new wife back to Fairacre to
live.

'We all thought he would,' was Mrs Pringle's comment.

Sitting on my spanking new garden seat, among the late
flowers of summer, I think of all that happened during my
last year at school.

I had known illness and fear, been obliged to make far-
reaching decisions, which I now knew were the right ones,
after the initial panic.

I had played my part in the hotchpotch of festivals,
fêtes, outings, quarrels and friendships which make up the
stuff of village life. New friends, as well as old ones, had

enriched my days, and I had the ineffable satisfaction of knowing that Fairacre school would continue to flourish.

As for Fairacre itself, for me it will always remain, as T.S. Eliot put it:

The still point of the turning world.

READ MORE IN PENGUIN

In every corner of the world, on every subject under the sun, Penguin represents quality and variety – the very best in publishing today.

For complete information about books available from Penguin – including Puffins, Penguin Classics and Arkana – and how to order them, write to us at the appropriate address below. Please note that for copyright reasons the selection of books varies from country to country.

In the United Kingdom: Please write to *Dept. JC, Penguin Books Ltd, FREEPOST, West Drayton, Middlesex UB7 OBR*

If you have any difficulty in obtaining a title, please send your order with the correct money, plus ten per cent for postage and packaging, to *PO Box No. 11, West Drayton, Middlesex UB7 OBR*

In the United States: Please write to *Penguin USA Inc., 375 Hudson Street, New York, NY 10014*

In Canada: Please write to *Penguin Books Canada Ltd, 10 Alcorn Avenue, Suite 300, Toronto, Ontario M4V 3B2*

In Australia: Please write to *Penguin Books Australia Ltd, 487 Maroondah Highway, Ringwood, Victoria 3134*

In New Zealand: Please write to *Penguin Books (NZ) Ltd,182–190 Wairau Road, Private Bag, Takapuna, Auckland 9*

In India: Please write to *Penguin Books India Pvt Ltd, 706 Eros Apartments, 56 Nehru Place, New Delhi 110 019*

In the Netherlands: Please write to *Penguin Books Netherlands B.V., Keizersgracht 231 NL–1016 DV Amsterdam*

In Germany: Please write to *Penguin Books Deutschland GmbH, Friedrichstrasse 10–12, W–6000 Frankfurt/Main 1*

In Spain: Please write to *Penguin Books S. A., C. San Bernardo 117–6° E–28015 Madrid*

In Italy: Please write to *Penguin Italia s.r.l., Via Felice Casati 20, I–20124 Milano*

In France: Please write to *Penguin France S. A., 17 rue Lejeune, F–31000 Toulouse*

In Japan: Please write to *Penguin Books Japan, Ishikiribashi Building, 2–5–4, Suido, Bunkyo-ku, Tokyo 112*

In Greece: Please write to *Penguin Hellas Ltd, Dimocritou 3, GR–106 71 Athens*

In South Africa: Please write to *Longman Penguin Southern Africa (Pty) Ltd, Private Bag X08, Bertsham 2013*

BY THE SAME AUTHOR

'Miss Read, as a country dweller, has been blessed with a love of nature, a taste for every one of the dramas with which rural life is fraught, and a sense of humour' – Elizabeth Bowen in the *Tatler*

Miss Read's books about village life are written with charm, humour and charity to delight readers everywhere.

NOVELS

Affairs at Thrush Green
At Home in Thrush Green
Battles at Thrush Green
Celebrations at Thrush Green
Changes at Fairacre
Farther Afield
Fresh from the Country
Friends at Thrush Green
Gossip from Thrush Green
The Howards of Caxley
The Market Square
Miss Clare Remembers
Mrs Pringle
News from Thrush Green

No Holly for Miss Quinn
Over the Gate
Return to Thrush Green
The School at Thrush Green
Storm in the Village
Summer at Fairacre
Thrush Green
Tyler's Row
Village Affairs
Village Centenary
Village Christmas
Village Diary
Village School
Winter in Thrush Green

OMNIBUSES

Christmas at Fairacre
Chronicles of Fairacre
Fairacre Roundabout

Further Chronicles of Fairacre
Life at Thrush Green
More Stories from Thrush
  Green

NON-FICTION

Miss Read's Country Cooking
Tiggy
Time Remembered